The County that Defiantly Sleeps

Stories from Clapford County Indiana

Simon C. McKim

Copyright © Simon McKim 2021
ISBN 978-0-578-83941-7
Ebook ISBN 978-0-578-84368-1

Thanks to anyone who heard or read one of these stories and offered comments: Jerry Koufeldt, Todd Dills, Allison Owen, NABC, Taco Steve, Pints & Union, the lovely audiences of Fireside Tales, supportive friends and family

Cover Design: Sarah McKim

simonmckim.com

Twitter @SimonMcKim

For Sarah, Rowan, Elspeth, and I guess even Barnaby
Tha gaol agam oirbh.

Foreword

Whatever on earth possessed you and made you pick up this book, I thank you for doing so. I can't think of a single sensible reason for you to have done this, but out of some sense of charity or out of some illness you have done it, and I am thrilled. For me this book is a labor of love and has taken more time than I care to admit. It's something I am proud of and nervous about. It isn't going to win any awards or make any lists, but it's in the world now and you're holding it. That is success enough for me.

Now that you're holding it, welcome to it! There are some things you should know about this book before it truly starts.

One thing is that it is a book about Hoosiers, written by a Hoosier.

When I was a kid we would go on trips all over the state of Indiana. My mother does genealogy, and at that time, before pretty much every headstone in the world was on the internet, you had to physically go to the cemetery to see what headstones said and get dates and other information, or you had to physically go to a library and look through microfiche to find what you were looking for. A lot of my childhood memories are of being in our minivan headed to this town or that town looking for long lost —very lost—relatives. For this reason, even though I was born in and have only ever lived in extreme southern Indiana, I have always felt like I grew up all over the state.

I'm a Hoosier. I grew up hearing poems by James Whitcomb Riley. I have read so much Kurt Vonnegut that I call him by first name now. One time I played "Let It Be" on Gene

Stratton Porter's piano. Another time in Shipshewana when I was a child, a little Amish girl saw me pee on a tree.

Speaking of James Whitcomb Riley, I have subtly tipped my hat to him in this book. If you ever have a chance to read the "Bear Story" by Mr. Riley, please do so, and read it aloud to children. I will never be able to read it or hear it without hearing my mother's impression of the bear.

As for Kurt, I have spent so many hours with his work I feel like he is an old friend. I doubt very seriously if we had ever met that he would have had much time for me, but I don't care. To me he is a very silly and a very important thing: a personal hero. A personal hero is someone you just love unabashedly and in spite of any input from your friends. Friends want to tell you about their personal heroes, their unabashed loves, and because this is an intensely personal and subjective thing, theirs never align with yours. We treat this as conflict and we shouldn't. It's not even a disagreement. I like green and you like yellow. Who cares? But, we all end up downplaying the importance of someone else's most important things so we can get to talk about our own. We rob one another of joy, in other words.

But back to Kurt, who is on such a pedestal for me, I have a bad habit of taking what he says as gospel, dogma, true without question.

Kurt said it, Q.E.D.

So I am going to tell you something I think is true, and I think it's true because Kurt said it in his foreword to the *Bagombo Snuff Box,* which is a collection of short stories:

A collection of short stories is just a series of Buddhist catnaps.

This is his punchline at the end of a discussion about how reading a short story is fundamentally different psychologically and physiologically from reading a novel, or watching television. There's nothing else like reading a short story, and I love them.

I can tell you for me there is nothing better for getting through the week than taking a Buddhist catnap: taking a few minutes to read a story. Nothing except perhaps a scotch on the rocks, but I find short stories are easier on the liver in the long run. Just imagine how different the world would be if all over on Friday nights you could hear "I need a Wodehouse, darling. I've had a hard week."

Anyway, the second thing you need to know is this book is a collection of short stories.

The third thing you need to know is that this book is, relatively speaking, clean.

There are people in my life who think I don't cuss. There are people in my life who know that's nonsense. Certainly the book in your hands is pretty clean. Not totally clean, but awfully clean. This is a stylistic choice and not a moral objection. I have no problems at all with swearing. In general I try not to do it though, and I'll tell you why.

When I was much younger, twenty-one or so, I sent off a short story to be published expecting it to go straight through to print due to my perception of my own natural brilliance. Instead I got a note back telling me to amp up the humor. To do this, I dumped a bunch of profanity into it, which doesn't make anything any funnier it just makes it dirtier. That story was eventually published but I can't for the life of me say why. Much of my writing from that part of my life was garbage. It was intensely superficial and chock full of profanity.

I was enamored with it.

Later in life, I was an open mic stand up comedian. I would guess in an average hour of being at open mic shows, I'd hear the F word 50 times. When you hear a word that much, it starts to hit you differently. You start to think about it differently. The power of it wears off and you see the mechanics of the way it's being used. It started to become clear to me that, for some folks anyway, it was a word used to compensate for weak material. A performer might as well wave a flag that says "this joke sucks but I have to sell it somehow."

There are of course comedians who use "bad" language who I would never say have weak material. The difference is those people could get by with clean language if they chose to do so, and the open mic-ers I'm talking about could not. For those good comedians, the content of the material and the skill at delivering it is good enough to succeed without any profane accoutrement. The other folks have only a hollow veneer of "edginess" that, like my twenty-something stories, has no depth. To me the litmus test became: could you succeed working clean?

I made a decision at this point to find out if I was any good, really. I banished profanity from my set.

I was not any good, it turned out.

It was a humbling realization.

In regular conversations, I find it to be unhelpful in establishing emphasis. I mean to say unhelpful in establishing the correct level of emphasis. If everything is effing this or effing that, there is no variation. You're already at ten, and you've left yourself nowhere to go when the situation really calls for a spectacular escalation.

So reverse Durkheim. The profane is sacred. It should be kept out of the everyday and reserved for special moments when it's truly called for. And when that moment comes, goddamn it, let 'er rip!

"Hang on a tick," you're thinking, "This is the way people really talk in the real world. In the interest of realism, shouldn't you replicate that?"

This is a fair question. I would say three things. First, all the objections above. Second, there are also people really in the real world who talk plainly without profanity. They should be represented as well. And like the good comedians who swear I spoke of before, the people in real life who cuss up a storm can turn it off from time to time, whereas the folks who don't swear can't turn it on...as easily. The clean position is the one accessible to everyone. It's more democratic.

Thirdly, one imagines that, from time to time, Romeo & Juliet had to poop. Shakespeare didn't bother to tell us about it. Perhaps Macbeth had hemorrhoids. We may never know. My point being, something can be a feature of reality without needing depiction. It could be depicted, but it's a choice to do so and not a necessity. So, I have made a decision in this book to try to keep it clean; not because it's more pleasant—there's plenty of unpleasant herein—but because pass or fail I want this to fly by its own wings, and not be appraised on arbitrary bases such as the number of "shits" that are in it.

-SCM

"And I love this place: the enormous sky, and the faces, hands that I'm haunted by. So why can't I forgive these buildings, these frameworks labeled Home?"

-John K. Samson, "This is a Fire Door Never Leave Open"

A Short History of Clapford County

In 1805 a caravan of intended gold prospectors left the Ohio River and traveled northwest into the interior of Southern Indiana. Their group was led by a man called Walter Clapford.

Walter was a small sweaty opportunist who'd heard about gold prospectors finding deposits all over the country and decided he would round up a group of people to head out west and form a settlement, collect a lot of gold, and relax in their newly created wealthy utopia. Walter took out advertisements in papers and spoke fervently at dinner parties, selling this dream to any who would listen. He gradually built up a small coalition to accompany him on his trip west.

His wife Sarah joined on the journey, although little is recorded of her. A few letters suggest she would rather have stayed home in the East with her family nearby where she could focus on doing a bit of writing. An open historical question is whether we were deprived of a great novelist by this journey, or whether she wrote later after settling in Indiana, but none of it was worth mentioning.

In early spring 1805 the party started west from Philadelphia. They picked up the Ohio River at Cincinnati and followed it on its northern side from there.

The settlers camped one night near what is now known as Lake Jefferson. When they woke up the next morning, the members one by one looked around at the soft rolling hills, the rich green forests, and the quiet clear lake, and one by one they decided they just couldn't leave this place behind.

It did factor into this decision, it should be noted, that the expedition was somewhat lost, having departed from the Ohio River to the south in an effort to explore what was rumored to be a large gold deposit in the Southern Indiana hills. This was a preview excursion for the gold they expected to find when they arrived at their big deposit somewhere west.

As they began to wander, they realized there are quite a lot of Southern Indiana hills, and they had no idea which hills were the right hills for unearthing this supposed gold deposit.

After three days of seeing only trees, some members of the party had doubts about Walter Clapford and his leadership, and shot off South to rendezvous with the River, never making it to the fateful night camped by Lake Jefferson.

The remainder of the group woke up on that fine morning, looked at their surroundings and claimed it must have been Fate that led them there. Men often find it comforting to claim that something grander is behind their absolute failures. It helps them save face.

The caravan settled right where they camped, and this settlement came to be the town of Hardy, county seat of Clapford County, Indiana. Because the company had brought enough provisions and munitions to get them through to California, they were well stocked in the first few months, and there was a bit less urgency in the early days of the settlement than there might otherwise have been.

Paths were found or made between the new settlement and civilization elsewhere, which opened up supply and trade lines to the rest of the world. Commerce began quickly.

Ezekiel Pemberton, the head of one of the leading families, took advantage of these new supply lines to set up a lumber mill, which quickly set him up as a financial powerhouse in the burgeoning community. Walter Clapford set up a bank, and then a small newspaper, so he could control all of both the information and money in the settlement. Inevitably, this led to the first Mayor of Hardy being won by Walter Clapford. This position, the position of Mayor, he held until his death.

The other people of Hardy were simple and poor. They formed small neighborhood communities near the heart of town where workers at the businesses in town lived. Beyond that, the settlers took advantage of rich soil in the areas outside the town to set up small farms that provided much of what was needed in town during its development.

Gradually new towns were formed outside of Hardy:

In 1862, a man called Matthias Tolliver founded a town in the northeastern swing of the county called Vicksburg. The Tollivers believed they had settled on top of a huge silver mine. It turns out there was no silver, but Vicksburg was home to a large network of natural caves. In future decades, these caves would become a national landmark.

Matthias himself spent his evenings and weekends exploring the caves in desperate search for silver. As there is none there, he never found any, however he did exhaustively document his searches, drew maps, and generated the single greatest resource for future explorers of the Vicksburg Caverns. It was rumored during his life that he used this extensive knowledge of the caves to help aid runaway slaves.

Some historians have positively stated that the caves were in fact used for this purpose, and it was for this reason that Matthias Tolliver spent so much time in the caves exploring and documenting rather than the quest for silver. There was certainly evidence found that some rooms in the cave were used for temporary lodging which lends some credence to the idea. However, critics argue this is consistent with a man staying too late exploring in the cave, and needing a place to sleep overnight. Chief among these critics are the eternally jealous Stancroft family.

When Matthias was not spending time in his cave, he spent his days as a tailor in town. He created suits for most of Clapford County, and his work was highly sought after. When Thomas and Hortense Pemberton were married, Thomas is quoted as saying "We couldn't get married without a Tolliver suit." This quotation, true or not, was circulated broadly and even used in advertisement in the Hardy Gazette.

Matthias' heir Bartholomew Tolliver took this business over and turned it into a fairly successful regional clothing company: Tolliver & Company. The newly branded company made overalls, dungarees and work shirts. Things that miners, farmers, and mill workers needed. In addition to these the company never gave up its flagship product: formal evening wear.

Tolliver & Company became immensely popular in the country and throughout the state of Indiana. Bartholomew felt that something should be given back to the community, and made a sizable donation to the Hardy Community College. The college's board of trustees felt they should use this opportunity to honor the Tolliver family in some way, and did this by creating the Tolliver Center for the Underground Railroad, forever cementing a connection between the family and the Underground Railroad in the eyes of many a local.

In 1910 the town of Valico was formed by Arthur Stancroft. In the very same year, Arthur founded Stancroft & Co. Arthur made denim work shirts and pants for miners. But as he was getting started in Valico, Bart Tolliver was getting started in Vicksburg. A formal accusation of espionage was made by Arthur Stancroft at the courthouse in Hardy. However the Tollivers had always been good and friendly neighbors to the Pembertons and Clapfords, which aided young Bart's case. The effect was that the accusation was simply laughed off. It was even satirized in a political cartoon in the Hardy Gazette where a businessman smoking a cigar was accusing an angel with wings and halo as being a thief.

The Stancrofts vowed to win in the end, but the popularity of Tolliver clothing grew and grew, and Arthur Stancroft grew more and more resentful as his clothing became widely described as "second-rate".

Economic reality sank in and the factory was shut down by Arthur's son David. The factory was later sold to John Clapford who turned it into the center of operations for the Clapford Printing Company. John Clapford turned the whole town into a "print house" town. So called because the houses were built quickly and cheaply with little to no variation to house the workers at the printing company.

The Stancrofts moved back to Hardy after the plant closed. David Stancroft founded a bank, and the whole family made transparent attempts to ingratiate themselves with the leading families in the county, specifically the Pembertons and Clapfords. It was generally regarded as off-putting. This along with the failed clothing business kept the family from being accepted into Hardy high society, despite being one of the original founding families of the county.

In 1940, a man called Patrick Turkelson bought a large parcel of land in the northwest corner of the county, and this parcel of land contained a coal deposit. When Patrick discovered this, mining in the Turkelson Mine began almost immediately.

Nearby the town of Steamsburg was formed by the miners who worked for Mr. Turkelson. Within ten years, all the coal in the mine was exhausted, it being not nearly as large a coal deposit as Mr. Turkelson initially had surmised based solely on wishful thinking.

The miners left town, and the entire economy of Steamsburg collapsed. The remaining population were the poor and purposeless who could not find work elsewhere, or did not have the means to pursue it, if they could find it.

As a result, Steamsburg remains one of the poorest communities in the state of Indiana, and the abandoned Turkelson Mines stand nearby as a monument to hubris.

In 1971, the church of the Generous Light of the Universe and Earth (GLUE) was created in Clapford county by a woman called Imogene Sneadly. GLUE rented land in the northern part of the county which is closed to the public and guarded by "No Trespassing" signs, razor wire, barbed wire, armed guards, and a pit bull named Harry. GLUE is a kind of gnostic religion which believes only certain folks should and do have access to truths about the universe, and as such, little is known about the religion. It is widely considered to be a cult. Beyond that not much is known, however a general core tenant of the religion can be found in Sneadly's treatise *The Principles of Transcending Bliss*, which argues that happiness is too feeble a feeling, and true meaning from the universe can only be found by going beyond happiness.

Of other history in the United States, Clapford County contributed very little. Many of the young men and women of Clapford went into the military. In terms of contributing soldiers, they gave their fair share, but there were no signs at the end of any towns proudly proclaiming this to be the home of this or that notable figure. Notability was a relative term, and residents tended to stay home and be notable compared to one another rather than trying to compete in the broader world.

From the founding of Hardy and establishing of Clapford County, through the decades down to today, the residents still hold on to their forbears' spirit of not having the initiative to move on from this place.

Josiah's Valley

When Josiah surveyed his new valley, there were no clearings anywhere, only treetops. The same oaks and maples and elms he'd seen everywhere else. A line of white branches and white trunks spoke of sycamores enjoying a waterway through the center of the valley.

If I build my home here, on the eastern shoulder, and facing the valley, the sun rise will behind the house every morning, and I'll watch the sunset over this valley every evening. I could build opposite-wise, with the home on the western shoulder and facing east, but I'll be to busy working to ever enjoy a sunrise, won't I? He was satisfied with himself and his own appraisal of his integrity. *It is proper*, he thought, *to build here.*

He began felling trees. It was slower work than he'd planned for. He had naively thought he'd swipe away the woods the way one shaves away their stubble. He wasn't prepared for the dull throbbing pain across his neck and shoulders, down his back and into his legs from swinging the axe all day. And he had certainly not considered that a tree will not fall in the direction you'd like it to fall simply because you wish it to be so. His first several trees fell in random directions, frightening Josiah. One started falling directly toward him. Luckily he'd had enough sense to run across the path of the tree, rather than try and run away from the tree.

"Don't you know to notch them trees?" A voice said.

Josiah wheeled around on the voice, holding his axe in a defensive posture, "Who's there?"

"The Sheriff, Mister Mathis. You can put down the axe. Don't see where you know how to use it too good anyway."

Josiah was squinting every which way into the woods, and still couldn't locate the source of the voice, "Show yourself."

"Good god man, I'm standing right here," the Sheriff took a step forward and Josiah finally saw him. He had been standing only a few yards away, "You never spent much time in the woods did you?"

"Not until I bought this land, no, but I'm learning."

"Are you now? Well that'll be good."

"What can I do for you Sheriff?"

"The Pembertons up the way lost a horse. I wondered if you'd seen one come through here."

"A Pemberton?"

"A horse!"

"Ahh. No. I don't think so. I've been very focused on the axe and the tree."

"Right. You're learning."

"Sir, are you mocking me?"

"No, Mr. Turkelson, I am not. Since you haven't seen anything, I'll have to continue my search elsewhere."

"I apologize that I couldn't give you a more definite report."

"Well," said the Sheriff. He backed into the woods and Josiah couldn't see him any longer.

He wiped his brow with his forearm and tried to imagine what notching a tree meant.

For supplies and sundries, Josiah rode his horse Maisie into the settlement at Hardy. Mr. Tolliver had established a small general store in the center of the town. It was a dusty, inconvenient place to go, but it was the only option for general supplies within riding distance for the entire area. Mr. Tolliver knew this, and his prices gradually rose accordingly.

Josiah was a naturally trusting man however, and he loved that store. On the Thursday after the encounter with the Sheriff at his new place, Josiah took his usual ride into town to visit Tolliver's and seek advice from others on handling the trees.

In the store his eyes fell upon a red-haired Welsh woman named Myffanwy. He thought she was the most beautiful woman he'd ever seen.

"Who is that person?" Josiah asked the clerk at the counter.

"She's Welsh," he said as if that were an explanation.

"What's her name?" he asked.

"Fanny," he snorted.

"Thank you. Do you know anything about her?"

"She's Welsh," he repeated.

"Is she married or...?"

"Don't know. She's Welsh."

"Well thank you just the same," Josiah said.

He decided to take matters into his own hands and just speak to the woman himself.

"Hello Fanny," he said.

"Who are you? I'll not be addressed as such. My name is Myffanwy."

"I'm sorry, you said 'Miv-an-we?'"

"No, Myf-fan-wy," she said slowly and clearly in a way Josiah did not find the least bit helpful.

"And you don't wish to be called 'Fannie'?" he asked.

"It's awfully rude, isn't it?" she seemed offended.

"Okay, Myffanwy it is."

"Thank you," she said sarcastically. She turned to walk away from Josiah.

"Uhh wait," he said.

"Mister, can I help you with something?"

"I was wondering if you'd do me the honor of taking a walk?"

"Mister, I've got to get this wire home to my mother."

"I can accompany you."

"It's too far."

"Oh, I don't mind."

"It's three miles."

"I can manage it."

"Well then, I suppose I can't stop you," she said.

Josiah walked with Myffanwy on her way home. He led Maisie the horse behind. They talked generally about life and family. Myffanwy explained her family had arrived from Wales in America when she was a baby, and had slowly drifted west until they settled here outside of Hardy.

Josiah explained his migration from Cincinnati after hearing the Clapford expedition had stopped here.

Along their way a rider approached from the opposite direction. As he got closer, Josiah recognized Walter Clapford.

Walter Clapford was the man who had led the settlers to this part of Indiana. He had founded the town, and the county was named after him. This he had done twenty years ago. Now He owned the bank in town as well as the newspaper. All the money and information in this little corner of the world passed through him. He was powerful. He dressed to express this power. He wore tailored suits and a little bowler hat. His facial hair was carefully cut for him into a meticulously neat goatee.

"Good afternoon Myffanwy, I see Mr. Mathis is walking you home."

Josiah looked at Myffanwy, surprised Mr. Clapford knew who she was.

"It's a free country, Mr. Clapford," she said, "I cannot stop him."

"Is he harassing you, Myffanwy?"

"I am not, sir," Josiah said, indignant.

"See that you don't," Walter said.

He rode past the two into town. Josiah and Myffanwy walked in silence for a few minutes.

"You know Mr. Clapford?" Josiah asked.

"Mr. Mathis please," she said, "I'd rather not discuss it."

"What is there to discuss?"

"He's been to our farm," she said, "He came to look at me."

"To look at you?"

"Yes, he likes to look at me. He thinks I'm beautiful."

"You are beautiful," Josiah said unconsciously.

"Thank you, but it makes me fearfully uncomfortable," she shuddered, "Father allows it. He means not to cause any disturbance in the town."

"I see," Josiah said.

After leaving Myffanwy at her parents' farm, Josiah mounted Maisie and rode back toward his valley.

The next week, Josiah made his customary trip into town, and again saw Myffanwy in the store. Josiah again offered to walk her home, and she again accepted.

This week, the two spoke of their love for one another. Josiah was surprised to learn he had made any impression on her, and vice versa.

They resolved to speak to her father when they arrived at the farm and Josiah would ask for her hand. Josiah was the most elated he had ever been.

Once again, they encountered Walter Clapford on their way. He took an exasperated attitude toward the two of them.

"Mr. Mathis, I told you last week never to harass this woman, and here I see you at it again."

"Mr. Clapford," he responded, "I'm sure your wife would be impressed to hear of your chivalrous interest in the affairs of my love's life."

"I beg your pardon?" he said.

"It's so noble of you to protect those that don't want your protection. Your wife must be proud."

"I don't know what you're insinuating sir," he said haughtily.

"We're to be congratulated, Mr. Clapford," Myffanwy said.

"Oh?" he said, "And why's that?"

"We're to be married," she said.

"Is that so?" he said.

"It is," said Josiah, brimming with excitement.

"Well," Walter said. He said nothing more. He prodded his horse and headed toward the town.

Josiah judged by his pace working on his land that his house would not be completed on time for the wedding, so he assembled a quick shack next to the place he planned to build the proper house. It was dismal, leaky and drafty. He hoped Myffanwy would not mind staying in it for a while until the house could be completed.

After the wedding, he considered whether he should ask for help from his father-in-law. He decided against it, feeling it might signal his weakness.

Myffanwy cheered up the place by her presence alone. It was an effect she was unaware of, sadly. From her vantage point, the place was in need of precisely what she brought to it. She worked hard to brighten it up and to encourage Josiah in his efforts at constructing the new home.

The going was slow for Josiah owing to his thorough lack of experience or knowledge, or even theory. He had simply an absurd confidence that as he went along the method for proceeding would unfold itself before him.

Months went by, some visible progress was made on the house, but it was agonizingly slow.

Fall was settling in, and the wind cut through the shack. Everything inside seemed to be in a perpetual state of damp. Even Josiah and Myffanwy's spirits began to dampen.

Still Josiah went to work on the house every day. He would alternate between chopping trees down to gather materials and adding those materials to the structure that was emerging.

One day the Sheriff found him at work chopping away at another tree, "You haven't learned to notch those trees yet?" he asked.

Josiah looked up and saw the Sheriff. He was pleased with himself that he had learned to spot a man standing in the woods. "Hallo Sheriff!"

"Could you set your axe down sir?" the Sheriff asked.

Josiah was a little confused by the request. It had been part of their protocol the last time they met, but it hadn't sounded so urgent that he put down the axe. He leaned the axe handle against the tree.

"I need to ask you some questions Mr. Mathis," he said.

"What's this regarding?" Josiah asked.

"I think you know well enough," he said.

"I don't."

"Can you give me an account of your movements yesterday?"

"I sure can," he said, "I was right here chopping this tree down."

The Sheriff laughed, "You were working on this same tree yesterday all day? And you still don't have it down?"

"It normally takes a couple days," he said.

The Sheriff laughed again, "No it does not! Do you expect me to believe that?"

"I beg your pardon, sir," he said indignantly, "It is the truth and I do not appreciate being made out to be a liar."

"Mr. Mathis, you have not to my satisfaction established your whereabouts for the time in question."

"I can give no other answer, sir. This is what I did all day yesterday. What is meant to have happened at the time you are inquiring about?"

"What color is your wagon?"

"My wagon?"

"Yes sir."

"It's red."

"Sir, we have reason to believe the Clapford County bank was robbed yesterday. A wagon matching the one you have just described was seen outside the bank at the time in question. And you have no alibi for your whereabouts."

"I have an alibi sir. I have given it to you."

"Josiah Mathis, you are under arrest."

Myffanwy came running out of the shack. From inside she'd been able to hear everything. "I can vouch for his whereabouts!" she yelled, "He was here all day yesterday, sir!"

The Sheriff turned to look at her, "It is a bit suspicious that you even know what we're talking about madam," he said, "It's as if you planned the whole affair and put your wife up to providing you an alibi."

"Sir, three things cannot be kept out of our home: rain, wind, and sound. I heard everything you said," she said. Josiah was embarrassed.

"Well that sounds like his handiwork," he said, chuckling.

"You see, sir, I heard your entire conversation and I can attest that Mr. Mathis has been here for the past two days working on chopping down this tree. He did not do what you say. He couldn't. He wouldn't."

"Be that as it may, madam, he has been arrested. Now he must go through the process of the law."

"Can't you just let him go?"

"Myffanwy," said Josiah, "I'll be redeemed. I have my innocence and incontrovertible proof. I can go with him."

"But who will go with me?"

"Go to your father's home. Explain what has happened."

"Good day, Madam," the Sheriff closed the conversation.

Myffanwy stood there in shock for some time watching the two of them amble off dutifully.

She absent-mindedly packed a few essentials from the shack, saddled up Maisie, and rode through town and beyond on the road to her parents' home.

She cried. She did not worry about the outcome of the case. It could only come out the way they had described. It was Josiah's compliance in the whole affair that worried her. He simply went along. She'd expected a scuffle: a little spark of manhood and fighting back.

That hadn't happened.

He had resigned himself to the inconvenience of the whole redundant affair, and he did it immediately. If it was going to come to nothing, what was the point in due process anyway?

When she arrived at the farm, her father asked if she had known he was out robbing banks in his spare time.

"He could not have done this. We have not been outside of earshot from one another since our wedding. I know precisely where he was the entire time," she replied.

"Still, where there's smoke there's fire dearie," her mother said, "There must be something to all of this."

"But there isn't," she rejoined.

"Well then the judge will find him innocent," her father said, "You have nothing to worry about."

"I just worry," she said.

"Why dear? Like you say, if he's innocent there's nothing to worry about."

"Because I have not told him yet that I am carrying his child."

Her parents processed this information for a moment before exploding in a shower of joy.

"You're going to have a baby!" her mother shouted.

"I'll have to shake his hand when he's freed," her father said.

"Oh dearie, I can see why you've been so worried about this! Of course he'll be cleared of this and all will be well again."

"Of course it will," her father added.

The trial of Josiah Mathis was a quiet affair. News of the robbery itself had only just made its way to the townsfolk via Mr. Clapford's newspaper. The paper, being owned by the same gentleman that owned the bank, took a rather dim view on the robbery, as well as the accused Mr. Mathis.

To read the story in print, you would have thought a guilty verdict and execution were foregone conclusions. Airtight damning evidence was reportedly found that put the case beyond the shadow of a doubt.

Everyone in the county was furious at Josiah Mathis, but none bothered to show up to the trial. They viewed it as a mere formality. They were clearing their calendars for the execution.

Myffanwy went. She was determined to give testimony and clear this all up. She came alone and sat behind her husband in the little courtroom.

The prosecution began by decrying the ignoble pursuit of bank robbery as a profession, and the dubious character of a man who would pursue it. Next the argument moved to the similarly dubious character of a man who would allow his pretty young wife to waste away living in a shack that couldn't keep out wind or rain.

Myffanwy watched Josiah's ears turn red. He was a lousy carpenter, but he still had his pride.

Such a man, the prosecutor carried on, would be capable of lying to an officer of the law the outrageous lie that for two whole days he'd done nothing but chop on a single tree that still hadn't come down!

Josiah let out what he meant to be a kind of indignant scoff that struck all who heard it as sounding rather like a gasp of terror.

"Furthermore," the prosecutor reached his climax, "the wagon seen leaving the bank with the money and robber inside was found at the accused's homestead."

This stunned both Josiah and Myffanwy. The defense assigned to Josiah stood to speak at his turn.

"Mrs. Mathis is here now and can positively attest to the accused's whereabouts."

"You can stop right there, Mr. Miller," the judge said, "I've no interest in hearing his wife lie for him."

Myffanwy stood up full of anger, "It's not lies. I speak the truth."

"Sit down Mrs. Mathis you have nothing to contribute today," the judge said.

Myffanwy sat down and felt the blood fall out of her body. Josiah turned to look at her in horror. The only proof of innocence was her testimony and it wouldn't even be heard.

The rest was played out as if choreographed. Every word, every motion, every second leading inexorably toward a guilty verdict.

Myffanwy did not hear any of it. She had retreated into herself to hide from the shock. Josiah sobbed. There wasn't anything they could do.

The judge sentenced Josiah to death by hanging the following Saturday. He was led away and Myffanwy just stared straight ahead not saying anything. Eventually she stood up and walked outside.

"This was a sham," she told Maisie on their ride home, "This was staged to give the death of a husband the appearance of justice. All of those heathens of this town, this wretched place, they will cheer. They will say how good it is to have this man off the streets. They won't think of me. They won't think of my baby. They certainly won't think of truth."

Myffanwy rode to the shack to collect more of her things. She took notice of all the things she had done to make the place cheerier, homier. They were pathetically inadequate. They made her feel as though she'd been made a fool of.

She collected her things and stepped out of the shack. Walter Clapford was standing there next to Maisie.

"Why are you here?" he asked her.

"Why are you here?" she asked him.

"Well, I'm the owner of this land. I came to inspect it."

"You are not."

"I will be once your husband is executed and the payments stop. I can foreclose then."

"It passes to me."

Walter laughed, "Are you going to make payments on the land?"

"And if I do?"

"I'll be surprised."

"Then expect to be surprised."

Josiah was to spend the next several days awaiting death. Everything had happened so quickly he hadn't quite understood all the moves until it was over and he was a doomed man. Then he had nothing but time to replay them over and over in his head, and marvel at the simplicity, the callousness, and intentionality of it all.

Myffanwy visited him daily. She did not know what to say to him. He did not know what to say to her. They mainly reminisced about their brief time together.

Josiah tried to remind her of his life's story so that she could tell it later. He found there wasn't much to tell. He stopped talking.

Myffanwy did not tell him about the baby. She thought it would be cruel to add to his troubles that he would never meet his child. Myffanwy just comforted him and they sat silently together.

Then she would leave and he would face the hours alone. He mused about their meaningfulness coexisting with their meaninglessness: every hour was numbered and precious to him now, and at the same time what did it matter to him what the time was?

"How are you going to pay for that land, Myffanwy?" her father asked her.

"I am going to have to find work or find a husband," she said.

"Myffanwy," he said. He paused and chose his words carefully, "Might it not be better to give up the land?"

"That's the Mathis family land now," she said.

"I know. I know. But might it be better to leave town? What is this place to you? Especially consider after he's gone."

"It's where you and mother are."

"If you were to leave this place, you could always visit us."

"Why should I leave?"

"How could you stay after what they've done to you and Josiah?"

"I mean to prove to them that I am stronger."

"That's fine dear, but what will that get you?"

"Their respect?"

"You should already have it. Why fight for it with the sort of people who don't grant it automatically? Why...why stay among people who would send your husband to the gallows just to separate you from him?"

She was stunned, "For what purpose?"

"I'm sorry, dearie, but it's better that you know," her eyes began to get angry before he'd even told it, "Mr. Clapford, he didn't like that you married that man. He wanted to go back to the days when he could come here and see you."

"So he arranged to have his bank robbed and then blamed it on Josiah?"

"Yes. It's just as you said."

"Then we must do something to stop him!"

"We cannot, is what I'm telling you. He owns the paper. He owns the bank. The judge is an old friend of his, so he practically owns the court. There's no where to turn from here.

"But from somewhere else, if you left here, you could get to him. You could get the newspapers to write about it when he doesn't own them."

Myffanwy mulled it over, "What about you?"

"We're stuck here, I'm afraid. I'm too old and settled to move."

"What about my baby?"

"Your mother can come and stay with you for a while. She can help you care for it."

The day of the execution came, and Josiah felt sick to his stomach all day. He tried reflecting on his life, but he'd done nothing else all week, and couldn't stay interested in the subject.

He found he couldn't focus on any particular thing, and couldn't settle on any position or activity either. He paced, he sat, he stood.

Eventually he was just impatient for the time to come. He wanted it to be over with.

Outside the jail, a gallows had been set up. Townsfolk began to gather. He could hear their chatter and the things they said about him.

One accused him of stealing children's toys at Christmastime. One accused him of philandering. One accused him of satanism.

They fed off one another and created more and more outlandish stories.

They were so ridiculous Josiah thought it was funny.

Eventually the time came. The Sheriff came in and asked if he was ready.

"Let's hurry and get it over with," Josiah said.

"It'll be the quickest thing you've ever done," the Sheriff chuckled.

Josiah laughed too, "I guess so," he said.

They walked outside and Josiah was walked up onto the platform. He looked around at the people who had gathered. There were thirty or so townsfolk gathered around cheering against the man and for the rope.

He saw Myffanwy standing away from the crowd. He looked at and started to mouth something to her, but the hood was placed over his head. All that had been discernible was "I."

The lever was pulled, the platform dropped out from under him, and Josiah was ended.

Myffanwy went home to her parents' house and spent the next week preparing to move. The following Saturday her father came to her inside and told her she had a guest.

"Walter Clapford is here to see you."

"What should I do?" she asked him.

"Talk to him I guess. But just in case, I am going to be cleaning my rifle on the front porch."

"Father!"

"I'll just have my eye on him," he winked.

Myffanwy walked out the front door and met Mr. Clapford on the porch. Her father followed with the rifle.

"Sir, I want no trouble," Walter said.

"Just needs a cleaning."

"Ah, well then," Walter said.

"Why don't we step away from the house a bit?" Myffanwy suggested.

After they'd walked out to the lane, carefully positioned in view of the porch, they stopped to talk.

"Have you worked out how you'll pay for that land?" Mr. Clapford asked, "I can't see why anyone would bother keeping it, to be honest."

"Oh you can keep that land," she said, "I won't need it. I'm moving away."

"You're moving?" he asked.

"Yes. I can't see much of a future for myself here in Hardy," she said.

"You can't move away," he said, "Otherwise what was this all for?"

"What was what all for, Mr. Clapford?" she asked innocently.

"I think you know damn well what I mean. You've been freed from that shack with that man who couldn't even chop down a tree. What sort of future did you see for yourself there? I did you a favor clearing him out of the way."

"You mean that you have another man's life on your conscience. You traded that life in for what ends up being no benefit to you just because you thought you had a right to me.

You must now live with this for the rest of your days. Now at least I have your confession thereof."

"What good does it do you if you have it?" he said aggressively, "The man's dead, it can't be changed now."

"True, and another paper in another town will be interested in hearing the details. Possibly your wife would like to know as well."

"No, you can't."

"Stop me," she said smiling, and pointed to her father on the front porch with the rifle.

"Well I never..."

"Please leave me alone, you dirty old man."

Walter Clapford spent the next weeks and months anxiously eyeing newspapers from out of town, but never saw a hint of trouble from them. He gradually began to relax and scarcely gave the matter any thought. New concerns occupied his attention as new concerns often do.

Seven months after moving to Bloomington, Myffanwy gave birth to Dafydd Josiah Mathis. Her new concern made the matter less urgent for her as well. She raised Dafydd with the story of his father, and asked that one day he take on the mission of exposing what happened.

He passed on to his son, and so on through the generations: a constant reminder to all that they had been cheated long ago, and something needed to be restored.

The Bear Slayer

Mrs. Applegate went in to Zeb's Diner with the juiciest piece of news she had heard in some time. The news she had heard concerned Kelvin the self-proclaimed "bear slayer" of Clapford County.

Kelvin had just sort of appeared one day and announced himself as the bear slayer.

"There haven't been any bears around here for a hundred years," Zeb said.

"That's what you say," Kelvin responded.

"Cause it's true."

After that he just kept coming back around to the diner, talking about his latest equipment purchases, his outdoor gear, guns, binoculars, and the like. All top of the line Macrotech equipment he spent money on. All to prepare for bear hunts.

He never mentioned going on one of these hunts, only the equipment he was stockpiling. It was obvious that he'd never really done any bear-slaying, but even in his own stories he seemed to confirm it.

Zeb harbored a special dislike for the man, and making fun of the bear slayer—the B.S.—was a favorite way to pass the lunch time rush in the diner.

On this day, Mrs. Applegate grabbed Zeb's attention, "Up in Steamsburg, someone said they saw a bear coming down from the north, headed south toward Hardy," Mrs. Applegate said, very pointedly gossiping in the Bear Slayer's direction, "Scared the willies out of some poor girl who'd gone off by herself to smoke a cigarette in the woods in peace."

"Oh really?" said Zeb, "What do you say Kelvin? Your county needs you. Go on out and get that bear."

Kelvin was noticeably fidgety. He kept sticking his hands in the pockets of his jackets, taking out whatever was in them, looking at it intently, and putting it back in his pockets. He was obviously avoiding eye contact.

"I uh," he stammered, "I guess I'm the man for the job."

"Great!" said Mrs. Applegate.

"I can't wait to see you bring it home," Zeb said.

Allison Flaherty was walking back from a hunt down to her home in Steamsburg. She hadn't seen any deer all month, and was starting to give up on finding some supplemental meat for her mother's home.

Since the miners had left and her father left with them, life had increased dramatically in difficulty while losing all of its complexity. There was only one objective now: survival. Before there had been boys and friends and school. There used to be dreams of a career and a beyond. That was back when the basic needs were provided for. It allowed a lot of brain power to be spent on other things. As species go, none is better at coming up with other things to worry about than ours.

Take away the provisions for the basic needs and life loses a lot of complexity. All of those other concerns become very low on the priority list. It's suddenly very simple and very much harder to deal with. Eat or die.

No more boys, no more career, no more social intrigue. Just survive.

She had hardened, as most folks in her shoes do. She took her father's shotgun, headed to the woods, and sought cheap meat.

This she had done all fall with no luck. On her way home through the woods she thought about what she was going to tell her mother, and she thought about the places she hadn't tried looking yet. There was a ridge over in the direction of Buffalo Bluff that she hadn't tried yet. No one ever said they saw anything over that way, but then why would they tell her where the deer were?

As she was walking she heard footstep sounds in the woods. Leaves crunching, sticks snapping. She stopped walking and became very still and quiet. She listened. She realized the shotgun was not loaded because she was walking with it and hadn't wanted to take any chances. Very smoothly, very quietly she reached into her pocket and pulled out a shell and without so much as shifting her weight to cause a leave to crunch, she loaded the gun and stood ready.

Meanwhile, the footsteps hadn't stopped or slowed down at all. They kept coming on, and they were coming from the South. There was a dense cluster of oak trees that cut off sight in that direction. She was blind, but whatever it was out there, it was bigger than a squirrel, and slower and clumsier than any deer.

Suddenly it started to whistle. Allison frowned. A human. Some damn fool was out here goofing around and whistling "On the Banks of the Wabash." That meant she wouldn't be able to come back this way on future hunts. It was now a place for tourists. Still, she held her gun up at the ready, aimed at the thicket of oaks. Human or not, she still didn't know she was safe.

Presently Kelvin stepped out from behind the woods, saw Allison standing there holding a shotgun on him, and stopped mid-whistle just as he was about to get to the part where the song says "through the sycamore the candle lights are gleaming." It felt incomplete, but there were more pressing matters at hand, he thought. Apparently he was being robbed.

"What do you want?" he asked, putting his hands in the air.

"I want you to stop whistling, for one thing."

"Sure. Will do. Absolutely."

"Now who are you?"

"I'm Kelvin the Bear Slayer," he said.

"There aren't any bears around here," Allison said, "not for a hundred years or so."

"You're welcome," he said, completing his customary joke, "No wait! There is one, actually."

"A bear?" she said looking at him like he was an idiot. She still hadn't lowered the shotgun.

"Yes. A lady saw one somewhere around Steamsburg."

"Well, we're somewhere around Steamsburg right now."

"I know," he said, "that's why I'm here. They sent the Bear Slayer."

"Okay. Then why are you whistling?"

"I'm whistling?"

"Just now coming through there you was whistling loud. You trying to scare off the bear?"

"Ehh no, I need to find it and ... eliminate it."

"All right," Allison said, still holding the gun on Kelvin, "you aim to shoot that bear?"

"Ehh well...how else do you get rid of a bear?"

"Where's your gun?"

"Fair question," he said, "I am kind of just trying to find it, I mean, the bear right now. Then I'll come back with my gun once I know where it is."

"Supposing you do find this bear right now," she started.

"Yes?"

"...and it ain't too pleased to see you. What then?"

"I don't follow."

"What if the bear attacks you, dummy," she said exasperated.

"Would they do that?" Kelvin asked.

"Well I can't speak for the bear, it if I were in her shoes I would."

"His shoes."

"What?"

"Never mind."

"Do you know how this bear got out here?"

"Well no," he said.

"I mean, what if it's a pet bear or a zoo bear that's just gotten loose?"

"Your point being?"

"What if you're going out to kill a tame bear that isn't going to hurt anybody?"

"Can bears be tamed?" he asked sincerely.

"I don't know," she said, letting the topic drift off into space.

"Can you take your gun off me?"

"I guess," she said, "you seem harmless. Dumb, but harmless."

"Well just because you're not a bear..."

"Move on," she said, "quietly."

Kelvin walked away carefully, reminding himself not to whistle, and stopping occasionally to look over his shoulder and see if he was being watched.

Allison headed for her house. She was replaying the conversation in her head, thinking about what a stupid person Kelvin must be wondering around in the woods after a bear, with no weapon and no plan.

Ahead of her she heard leaves rustling and sticks snapping again, but she knew the master bear slayer could not have gotten here already. Something new, she thought. She stopped moving again, got very quiet again, and checked her shotgun to see if it was still loaded. It was.

Through the trees she caught sight of a black bear. So Kelvin wasn't lying, she thought, which means he's an honest idiot anyway. The bear hadn't seen her, but it also stopped moving, sniffed the air, and began to look around.

She knows I'm here, Allison thought, in a minute she's going to be here, what should I do?

The bear decided the scent it had detected was coming from Allison's direction. It started moving her direction very quietly. Allison remembered the conversation about the bear being tamed, and she thought that was her best hope, the best case scenario, so she hoped for it. She decided to wait and see how the bear reacted to her before doing anything rash.

The bear just seemed curious about her. It was walking slowly, looking in her direction, trying to gather as much information as it could. It did not seem like an angry bear, and it did not seem to be defending its territory or its cubs.

The bear finally approached Allison and sniffed three quick sniffs. Allison could see the bear was in fact a female. The bear starting walking in a circle around her, sniffing here and there, and generally just getting a good eyeful. Allison lowered the shotgun. Here was someone she could trust more than any bear slayer.

Gradually the bear moved closer and closer to her, not menacing. Just curious.

She decided to take a step forward. The bear paused and turned her head to look at Allison. Then she adjusted her route and walked in a new circle around Allison's updated location.

So Allison took another step. Again, the bear paused, and made another minor course correction.

Gradually the two of them were walking slowly together, with the bear circling Allison, sniffing the air here and there. Allison carried on this way until she got to her home at the edge of the woods. The bear stopped at the house, and stood up on her hind legs. She looked around agitatedly, sniffing the air over and over. There was something about the house she did not care for.

Allison had hoped by the time she got home she would have come up with a plan for what to do at this point, but during all the long walk, nothing had come to her. Still, this stopping, standing, and sniffing seemed to go against whatever the plan might have been.

"Meryl!" a voice shouted in rebuke. The bear got back down on all fours and seemed to relax again.

Allison turned to face the voice and saw an older black gentleman in a suit he'd obviously owned for a while. It showed wear around the shoulders and pockets. His pants hung baggy around his ankles and dragged along the ground. He had two days' growth of beard and a fedora that looked as if it had been stepped on. Both he and Allison looked at each other with exactly the same question, "Why does this bear obey that person?"

"Thank you for finding my bear," he said.

"She found me, sir."

"She followed you home. That is very strange. And you held your calm: very impressive."

"She wasn't aggressive, so I didn't have any reason to be scared."

"I'm Miles Coontz," he said.

"Allison Flaherty."

"Irish," he noted.

"I don't know, honestly," she said.

"Well, anyway, I work for a circus passing through to Louisville. We're supposed to be there this whole week, but Meryl and Pete got away from us."

"They broke out of their cages?"

"Oh no. They're both very good—better than most people I'd wager—so we let them loose when we stop, if there aren't any people around. They usually just linger with us and don't stray or anything. I guess I took it for granted and they got curious and got separated from us and we just couldn't find them anywhere."

"So you have another lost bear around here?"

"Yes, the male. Pete we call him."

"Then you should know there is a man who calls himself a bear slayer out there in the woods. I ran into him right before I ran into Meryl."

"Golly, then we're racing against the clock. I've got to find Pete before this bear slayer does."

"I don't know that he's really much to be worried about. He didn't strike me as being too educated on how to handle himself."

"That's worse!" Mr. Coontz said, "If he doesn't know how to handle himself and he gets spooked..." he thought for a moment, "Ms. Flaherty, I'll pay you."

"For what?"

"Well the circus is going to give you reward money for Meryl anyway, but if you can get Pete back here too, alive and safe, I'll triple it. How does nine hundred dollars sound?"

Nine hundred dollars was a lot to her. She could feed herself and her mother for months and months. I might even be enough to let her life get a little less simple for a while. It was enough to change her life, if all the cards fell the right way.

"Yessir I'll do it. Only I'll have to start out in the morning. It's getting dark, I have to feed momma and do chores."

"There's no time to wait until morning. What about this bear slayer?"

"You're safe from him. He definitely can't find a bear in the dark. Anyways, even if he did, he doesn't have a weapon."

"You mean to tell me he went out into the woods after a bear without a weapon?"

"Sure did."

"You're right. We *don't* have to worry about this one tonight. Go take care of your momma and then find my bear tomorrow. I'll be waiting here for you when you and Pete come back."

When Kelvin left Allison in the woods, he was no less nervous about the prospect of encountering a bear. He wandered around in the woods and even returned to whistling to try and help calm his nerves. He even imagined the bear might be scared off by it. Of course if he had known the bear was accustomed to being around humans, and probably wouldn't be scared off by whistling, he might not have whistled.

He took no advantage from his Macrotech compass, binoculars, or maps. He let all the equipment he had spent so much investing in dangle at his sides. He walked in what he imagined was a big circle, hoping to find his truck and just go home for the night on the pretense that he really did need his gun if he was going to run into the bear out there. The girl hadn't convinced him of that, he told himself, it was a decision he came to on his own.

But not using his compass, he'd made an error trying to circle back around. The big circle he walked in was awfully big. Much too big for Clapford County to contain. More of a curved line really. It may have eventually circled all the way around, after including a bit of Kentucky and possibly even a little Illinois, but that was never to be.

He walked all the way to Buffalo Bluff in about three hours. He stared up at the town overlooking everything in the county, and realized his mistake. He was losing the sun, and he knew he'd never make it completing his circle, now that he realized how big it was. So he decided to just go back the way he came.

He pulled his branded Macrotech flashlight out, flicked it on, and marched off into the darkening woods.

Kelvin did not take the way he had come on his way back. It worked out in his favor, he more or less walked a straight line back to his truck. He was not aware that was what was happening however, and he became increasingly concerned that he did not recognize anything along the way back. He took some brief comfort in telling himself that there was daylight earlier, he was looking at trees from the opposite side, and the flashlight probably created some eerie, unnatural shadows.

That worked for a few minutes and then he was right back to whistling the "Battle Hymn of the Republic."

He began to suspect he was being followed in the woods. He was not, but he imagined someone much more adept at navigating the woods was walking behind him, able to conceal themselves better than he was, whistling and waving a flashlight around. His pace quickened and then quickened some more.

He paused here and there on the way to catch his breath, since he was going so fast. In one small clearing he looked around at the trees and noted to himself that he must be on the right track. This is where he met that girl earlier.

It was not the same clearing. He was about a quarter mile off course from that clearing. This information was of no consequence. Kelvin felt relieved he was headed the right way, and in a manner of speaking he was.

After an hour and a half from the turnaround point, he was back at his truck in Steamsburg. He was surprised with himself at how expertly he had found his way back. Perhaps he was really as expert an outdoorsman as he told everyone he was. Had he spoken it into existence? Maybe so, he thought. He drove home and crawled into bed confident that in the morning he would head out and kill himself a bear.

Kelvin woke up late the next morning very hungry. He got all of his outdoor gear together, including his shotgun, loaded it all in his truck and went to Zeb's for a fortifying brunch on his way to spend the day in the woods.

Zeb was grinning a monster grin when Kelvin came in, "If it isn't the bear slayer!" he chortled, "Our hero!"

"I'll get it today," Kelvin said calmly.

"Well you'd better," Zeb responded.

"I'll have the breakfast special."

"Did you hear some girl up in Steamsburg caught one of the bears?"

"Bears?" Kelvin tried to process all the new information he was receiving at once, "There's more than one bear? And one of them was caught? By a girl? Which girl?"

"I don't know which girl. Hank over at Felson's told me when he delivered this morning. He saw a girl walking out of the woods with a bear following her. She handed it over to this fella. Someone heard him say he needed her help with the other one. So there must be more than one."

"I better hurry and get that other bear," Kelvin said resolutely trying to hurry on his food.

"Hang on a second there bear slayer," Zeb said, "Sounds like these bears belong to somebody. You better not go out killing somebody's bear," he chuckled, "Especially if it's the kind of somebody who owns more than one bear."

"They can't be tamed," Kelvin said, taking a stand where he definitely wasn't sure, "They're dangerous. If they can't be caught they've got to be taken down."

"And you're the man for the job?"

"Who else is there?" he said dramatically.

_--_*

Allison spent her morning walking more or less aimlessly in the woods. The potential area Pete could be in was enormous, and she wasn't sure how to narrow it down. She thought a reasonable approach was to go to the clearing where she'd met Meryl and try to follow her path from there backwards.

It made sense to her that the two would have been together for a while at least, so backtracking her path could lead to wherever they had gone their separate ways.

This approach had not proven fruitful. She lost Meryl's trail almost immediately, and attempting to take the path and direction she was moving in when she'd found her and extending it straight out had been a dead end as well, as it led into a bramble wall of wild multiflora rose bushes.

She felt that, like Edison, she hadn't failed, she'd found so many ways that didn't work. She narrowed down the forest to a particular quadrant Pete was likely to be, at least: the southeast quadrant in the direction of Valico. She walked in that direction, hoping to pick up the trail.

She decided to deploy a secondary strategy as well: she began periodically dropping a gumdrop on the ground where she walked. She hoped Pete would sniff these out and follow them right to her. If he did that, he ought to be easy to lead home with whatever gumdrops were left.

As she went she thought about what would be the best to do with the nine hundred dollars. It was almost enough to buy food for a whole year. After the year was up, of course, you had to think of what happens after that. Maybe it was enough to enroll in a typing course. She could get work in Hardy and provide more long-term stability for her family, if she could type. That would be enough for them to climb one rung of the ladder. That would be enough, she thought.

She continued in this daydream of the future for several hours, walking a kind of radio wave pattern through the woods from the furthest east you could go and still be considered in the southwest part of the woods all the way to the eastern edge and back, moving gradually south as she went.

She was just beginning to allow herself to imagine love in her future when she head a shotgun go off. She came crashing out of sweet dreams of the future suddenly. The shot was close by.

Ordinarily there wouldn't be anything that strange about hearing a gunshot during deer season, but word got around that there was a bear in the woods, and most of the hunters in Clapford County suddenly found there were other chores they could be doing this morning that were probably a higher priority than hunting today. No, they protested, they weren't afraid of any bears, it's just that these sock drawers aren't going to organize themselves.

This was the first shot she'd heard all day, and she worried that Pete might have been involved. She ran in the direction the sound had come from.

She heard Pete give a low moan, "whoooom," and she feared the worst.

She popped out of a clearing and saw Pete standing on his hind legs in front of a tree, and against the tree was pressed Kelvin the Bear Slayer. He was armed today, she noticed. His right hand was holding the shotgun and waving it around helplessly in the air. Pete swiped with his right paw and swatted the gun away from Kelvin.

"PETE!" Allison yelled, trying her best to mimic Mr. Coontz when he yelled at Meryl the night before.

The bear looked at her and sat down on his haunches. Kelvin looked at her with sheer terror and confusion on his face. Only the blink of an eye ago this bear was holding him against a tree and now it was docile and sitting on the ground in front of him. Very close in front of him, but docile, for now.

"So they can be tamed?" he asked.

"Did you shoot this bear?"

"I-I-, I fired."

"I heard that, did you hit him?"

"I don't think I did."

"Good. Now, before I let this bear loose on you again," she bluffed, "get out of these woods for good."

"Okay I'll just pick up my shotgun."

"No you won't!" she shouted.

"But that's my property. I'm not leaving it out here in the woods! Do you know how expensive that Macrotech gun is?"

"I'll return it to you. It's your gun. But I'm not giving it to you until we're out of the woods, and this bear is safe from you."

"But I'm-"

"I don't care what you are. Go before I let Pete knock off more than your firearm."

He glanced at the bear, and took off running into the woods.

Allison and the bear took each other in for a couple of seconds. The weight of the moment had passed, and it was starting to dawn on Allison that she had done it. The money would be more than just in her imagination. She was going to take that typing class, get a job, provide for her mother, find love, all of it. She cried.

She walked slowly around Pete, and saw no signs of injury. Not only was Kelvin a terrible outdoorsman, he was also a terrible shot. She took a gumdrop out of her pocket and tossed it onto the ground in front of Pete. He lapped it up with his tongue and got up on all fours, ready to follow this new provider of sweets.

The Stancroft Plan

Oliver Stancroft had a new plan to ascend the Clapford County social ladder and dominate the other families. Class politics in Clapford were real. Money mattered, of course, but being in one of the so-called "founding families"—the Clapfords, the Pembertons, the Stancrofts, the Tollivers, and the Turkelsons—was practically essential to really and truly be somebody.

Within the founding families there was a hierarchy as well. Clearly one of them got their name on the whole county. The Stancrofts looked down on everyone, especially those you might rightly call their betters. The Pembertons--wealthier, more charitable, more polite, and better liked--were special objects of hatred. Far worse than the Pembertons were the Tollivers who the Stancrofts considered their equivalents. The Stancrofts saw so much of themselves in the eyes of a Tolliver it was impossible not to hate the entire clan. It was a feud that went back generations. At one point, both the Stancrofts and Tollivers had started clothing companies, and when the Tolliver company became more popular, the Stancrofts accused them of corporate espionage. It was a laughably false accusation, which compounded the shame of the failing company.

In the eyes of all of the other families, the Stancrofts were last in the pecking order up until the sad business with John Francis Turkelson marred their family name. The Stancrofts of course saw this as a sleight, one that burned deep into the ancestral marrow and kept the blood simmering, ready to boil over at any moment.

Oliver Stancroft set upon strategy after strategy to reduce the lot of the other families to "rags and ashes, rubbing oak branches through their hair." He said it with such glee and purpose his children thought it sounded wonderful without being able to penetrate to the meaning of the joyful words. They frequently bragged at school about making everyone rub oak branches through their hair. As they got older and the meaning of those words was understood, they still thought they sounded gleeful and innocent.

Jefferson Pemberton the younger could only benevolently grin at the hubris. His father, the elder Jefferson Pemberton had told him about the Stancrofts over dinner one evening, "They are good people. They only have bad ideas."

Mr. Pemberton believed the thing many exquisitely wealthy men have the luxury of believing when they only meet friends and don't feel threatened in the slightest: there is no reason why anyone should have anything but positive feelings about everyone else, at least outwardly.

Over the years there were several plans. The first was claiming that William Clapford had offered to sell his daughter Mathilda to Oliver to be married. This was so laughably false that when Oliver made this claim in front of people for the first time, they all assumed he was joking and it got a big laugh. People shared it as an example of Oliver's good sense of humor for years. In fact, it scarcely bears mentioning as a plan to take the Clapfords down, except that after this happened, William paid for Mathilda to visit Chicago for a summer. She never returned from this trip. By all accounts, she is quite happy living in Evanston, teaching Biology at Northwestern. In no one's eyes was there a connection between Oliver Stancroft and Mathilda leaving town, but one pair of eyebrows was raised.

After this were a string of accusations of espionage, that someone had been paid to break into the bank of Stancroft and Sons, rifle through some papers, and put everything back neatly. These too were barely given any notice. They only generated in others a general sense that Oliver Stancroft was paranoid, and somewhat tiresome.

Oliver's new plan began innocuously enough at breakfast one morning, "Where is my coffee mug?" he asked.

His wife Beverly looked at him confusedly, "Which mug?" She was thinking of the fifty or so mugs in their kitchen cabinets, and whether now her life's task was to be keeping track of each of them.

"The Nixon mug."

One fall Oliver had found a coffee mug in a vendor's stall at Hardy Harvest, the town's annual fall festival. The mug was ugly—tan brown with a mustard yellow moose drinking out of a lake. On the opposite side was a list of *some* of America's National Parks: Yellowstone, Yosemite, Dry Tortugas. The rim was chipped, making a triangle pointing down between the moose's antlers. The woman running the stall told him that particular mug had once--but only once--been used by Richard Milhouse Nixon, erstwhile president of the United States. She could not say at what point in his life he used it, but think of it's resale value, she hinted, and for only twelve dollars!

Oliver first thought of the substantial profit, and perhaps the smell of popcorn from the Harvest food court reminded him of playing youth league baseball as a child, and perhaps that comforted him and lured him into a sense of purpose and adventure, because the idea that he might need some way of proving that this mug was once used by Nixon in order for it to be worth anything completely escaped his notice. All he managed to say at the time was, "Can you break a twenty?"

His initial plan for the mug was just to resell for profit. He re-thought on his way home and decided it might come to some social advantage for the family. Some way or other they could use the mug to ascend the Clapford hierarchy. Perhaps it could be donated to a museum, or kept and used as a conversation piece. He even entertained the idea of finding a whole series of similar objects and establishing his own museum.

To do any of those things he would need to establish the authenticity of the mug, and prove its provenance, so it was best to hold on to it.

He started by searching the internet for Nixon coffee mugs hoping to find a picture of the mug being used by Nixon. Instead his searches yielded a lot of merchandise with pictures of the former president printed on them. He did find some pictures of the president drinking coffee, but the mugs were classier, more what you'd expect to see a head of state drinking from, not the ghastly beaker he'd brought home.

He also thought that, come what may on the authentication front, and whatever purpose he'd use the mug for, he was going to need some good photographs of the mug. Especially if the purpose was to sell it. He found the best lighting was in the room off their garage. He took the mug out there, set up a solid colored backdrop and took several photographs of the coffee cup.

That potentially valueless mug was now missing, and he took the opportunity to remind his wife of its irreplaceability, "Do you have any other mugs Nixon used?" he asked her.

"Did you look in the dish washer?"

"Of course I looked in the dish washer!" He bellowed, "I've looked everywhere!"

"Obviously not," she said, "or you would have found it by now."

"Perhaps one of those Tollivers broke in here and stole it," he said, "Maybe it's real! Maybe Nixon really did use it, but it proves some kind of conspiracy! Something involving Clapford County, and that's why they don't want me to have it."

"Who?"

"How can you ask me who? Take your pick! Clapfords! Tollivers! Pembertons! I imagine they're all involved somehow. As long as they have power, they'll stop at nothing to keep a Stancroft down."

"You sound crazy, dear."

"Well, where's the mug?" he said, resting his case on that.

That morning, Oliver drove to the office, not listening to the radio. He was imagining the mug had led to a breakthrough of enormous national interest. He pictured some journalist interviewing him, and he was attempting to appear wise, "it all started, you see, when I noticed my prized coffee mug—used by none other than Richard Milhouse Nixon, mind you—my coffee mug had gone missing. Who would take a man's prized coffee mug unless they had something to hide..."

He arrived at the office convinced something was up, something sinister and hidden, something that needed light shined on it. He resolved to keep it quiet however, until he had more information. The weight of what he assumed he would uncover was too great for idle Hardy gossip.

Oliver had a teller, David Thompson, an unambitious, timid man by all accounts. He did not seek to deal with loans any longer, clerking was fine by him. He had practiced law earlier in his career, feeling compelled to do so by the expectations of society and in particular his parents. It was more than he could cope with psychologically. He left the law behind and started at the bank as a loan officer. Once his parents passed, he asked for a smaller role in the bank. Oliver was surprised. He wasn't aware that a smaller role was possible, "I suppose you could be a teller for me..."

"That'd be perfect."

That was twelve years ago. During all that time, David had learned to read Oliver's facial expressions pretty well. He could tell when his boss was disappointed, and he worried about it for days each time he was.

This morning the face told a familiar story: they're out to get us, but we're in the right, and we've got a plan.

"Oliver, what have they done this time?"

"Who says they've done anything?"

"Your face, I know that look. They're up to something."

Oliver sighed, "Look, I really can't talk about it."

"What? You?" David was surprise, "You can't talk about it?"

"No I can't. What's so shocking about that?"

"Oh my... are they pressuring you to be quiet about something?"

"What? No, of course not..."

Oliver walked into his office and shut the door.

Oh my god, thought David, *they really are putting the squeeze on him this time!*

David Thompson went home to his wife Daisy that evening and told her there really was something big going on this time. Oliver wouldn't even speak of it, so they must have something on him. All of his talk about the Pembertons and the Clapfords and the Tollivers and the Turkelsons might actually be legitimate.

Daisy resolved not to speak of this any further to avoid spreading any gossip. But the next day she went to her work at the Hardy Savings and Loan, where she was the Branch Manager. Under normal circumstances, she'd entertain her employees with whatever tale her husband had heard from Oliver Stancroft whenever they came up. If nothing came up, she didn't mention him.

This day, she had a meeting with the local taxidermist Martin Stanhoover about a loan for a brick and mortar shop. Martin in particular had an ear for the gossip of Hardy's high and mighty. He loved to hear whenever Daisy had a story that came from Oliver Stancroft, "What's new with the Stancrofts?" he asked.

Daisy balked at a reply, "Oh I...I wouldn't know."

"Wait...what?"

"Nothing, there's nothing going on over there."

"Oh but there's always something going on over there."

"No, not especially this time."

"You paused you know. Like there is something..."

"Let's just drop it and discuss your loan?"

"Oh, yes!" Mr. Stanhoover was happy to move on.

After Martin left the bank, he walked over to Alice's Diner for lunch with a group of guys he met every week there.

"What's the matter Marty? Didn't you get your loan?" asked Jim.

"Oh, sure, sure I got it," he put on a smile.

"So why do you look so confused? Wondering why they'd give you any money?"

"Well, it's the strangest thing, normally over at the bank Daisy tells me what wild theories Stancroft has going on...but this time she didn't."

"Maybe there aren't any."

"No she made it seem like there was something going on, something she was even worried about, but wouldn't speak on."

"You mean, they're really out to get him like he says?"

"Don't know..." said Martin. But the idea that they were was now planted in a dozen or so brains. One of those brains belonged to Lyle Hoover.

Lyle had a reputation in town for letting the cat out of the bag. If you wanted a secret kept, you made sure Lyle didn't know what it was. If you were looking for a confidant, and you landed on Lyle, you could be sure you had made a miscalculation somewhere along the way.

He was an otherwise fairly ordinary Hardian: he liked basketball, he worked for Tolliver & Company, he went fishing on weekends, and he imagined himself to be more a man of integrity than was probably fair.

Lyle went back to work that afternoon very affected by what he'd heard. Could it be the Tollivers were actually conspiring against the Stancrofts? It didn't sit right with him. He didn't know if he cared to work for people who would do that sort of thing to other folks. Whatever sort of thing it was. Nobody seemed to know any details, but it sure must be underhanded, he thought.

He went straight in to Chelsea Tolliver's office when he went into the building.

"What's going on?" he said as he walked up to her desk.

She took a long guarded look at him. She was honestly perplexed at what he might be asking about. Usually if there was some kind of policy change in the company she could expect Lyle to ask about it. There hadn't been any, and sales were steadily increasing. There were no concerns looming about either job losses or long stretches of overtime, "Everything is business as usual, Lyle," she said, "so I'm not sure I know what you mean.

"Oliver Stancroft...what's going on with him?"

"Oliver Stancroft? At the bank? I don't work at the bank. Lyle, what are you talking about?"

"At lunch today, they were saying something hush-hush was going on with Oliver Stancroft."

"Ahh, well if it's hush-hush I don't see how I could know about it."

"Someone is putting the screws to him."

"Oh he says that about every five days. Someone ought to tighten his screws. He's got one loose."

"Chelsea I mean it sounds serious this time."

"Did you have lunch with him?"

"Ehh, no. Some friends meet up for lunch and Marty Stanhoover came in saying something was up."

"I see so this is secondhand information. What did Marty tell you Oliver Stancroft said?"

"That's just it, he wouldn't say. I mean, Oliver wouldn't say. You know he's always got a story, but when even he's bothered so much he can't speak, well...you see? It makes seem more real."

"I can assure you Lyle, as far as I know there is nothing going on."

"I appreciate it, Chelsea. I just... I just don't think I could work for somebody working underhandedly to take a fella out at the knees."

"I assure you I'm not."

"I sure hope that's true," he said, and then walked out of her office.

Chelsea spent that evening calling folks she knew in the other founding families to feel them out for information about what Lyle had said. She just wanted to confirm what her heart already told her was true. That there was nothing going on, and this was all a lot of nonsense. Predictably, she found nothing. All of the families had heard similar rumors that day, and everyone was curious. The Pembertons and Clapfords weren't sure who people were even talking about. The Turkelsons wanted to know what she wanted to know: what was it he was claiming had happened. She had to inform them there had been no actual claims made. Nobody had any new information. Now she was sure it was nothing, even if she couldn't exactly prove it.

The next evening, Lyle Hoover rang the doorbell on Oliver Stancroft's front porch. He'd combed his hair over with thick pomade and put on a dark green wool blazer with a brown overcheck pattern and baggy khakis that were a bit too short for meeting an Oliver Stancroft. He did not look nice, but he *did* look like someone who was trying to look nice, and that was charming in its own right.

Charming or not, he felt silly. The effort he'd put in to this costume represented a gamble to Lyle. He was trying to show respect to the family he was visiting by dressing as best he could, but he feared he'd overdone it, or simply gone in the wrong direction. He felt ridiculous and his ears burned bright red.

Beverly Stancroft came to the door, "Lyle Hoover," she said, surprised, "I wasn't expecting you this evening. What can I do for you?"

"Ma'am," he said apologetically, "I came to speak with Mr. Stancroft. Is he in?"

"Is he expecting you?" she asked.

"I...uhh...no. No, he's not. I just hoped he had time for me this evening is all. It's a matter of importance to me, but perhaps none to him."

Beverly Stancroft eyed Lyle for a moment and stepped back to usher him in, "I'll see. Please wait in our sitting room for a moment." She led him to the second door inside the house, and gestured for him to have a seat.

The Stancroft sitting room was an oppressive expression of vanity. There was a kind of desperation betrayed by the decor: oil paintings of relatives, a large globe on a cherry stand that came to waist-high on Lyle, and four beautiful leather armchairs. Whoever the decorator was, they certainly wanted to leave any visitor with an unmistakable impression when they left this room.

Lyle wondered if all the wealthy people in town had rooms like this in their house, and if this was something he was really sad was missing from his own home, or if he wasn't a little relieved to not have to acquire all of this furniture.

After another minute or two Oliver Stancroft came in wiping his hand off on his shirt. Lyle was a bit disappointed to see Oliver in a t shirt, and one that he treated so cavalierly.

"My wife says you're wanting to see me," Oliver said, extending his hand for Lyle to shake.

Lyle took his hand, "It's a matter of importance to me," he said, "though it may be of no consequence to you."

"Well, let's see if I can help set your mind at ease," Oliver day in one of the leather chairs and motioned to Lyle to do the same.

Lyle was relieved. He'd felt ridiculous standing all this time, but taking a seat had seemed like a liberty he couldn't take. "It's about my employer, sir."

"And who's that?"

"Chelsea Tolliver," Lyle said.

"It's WHO?" Oliver boomed, standing up from his chair.

"Sir, please be seated. I know the history. But listen, I've heard this rumor, and I can't bear to work for her if it's true. So I wondered what you could tell me."

Oliver remained standing, "Firstly, you *shouldn't* bear to work for that family. Secondly, I don't know what the rumor is. Let me know and I'll share what light I can share."

"Thank you. Well, I can't say what the story is. I don't know it."

"What?"

"Well, all I know is there's a rumor that something is going on, that the other families are doing, and you're so worried about it you can't speak."

Oliver immediately thought of his lost Nixon mug, "But you don't know what."

"Right."

"They're always working on something to try and hold me back. I don't know what you're referring to, but I know just recently an important artifact was removed from my home. I have my suspicions about who the culprits are."

Tears welled up in Lyle Hoover's eyes. This news had struck just the wrong chord in him. "She lied to me," he said.

"She lied to you?"

"She said she knew nothing about this. How could that be true?"

"I can't answer that," Oliver Stancroft said. He wondered briefly if he'd led Lyle to draw some pretty specific conclusions he wouldn't have come to on his own. At the end of the night he comforted himself with a bourbon and vaguely saying that where there was smoke there must be fire. He just needed to know what was burning.

The next day Lyle Hoover quit his job at Tolliver and Co. in quiet, pointed fashion: he once again barged into Chelsea

Tolliver's office and said, "I cannot in good conscience continue to work for this company knowing what I now know."

"Know what about what? We've been through this, there's nothing going on."

"I heard a different story from Oliver Stancroft," he said.

"Let me get to the bottom of this," she said.

"Get to the bottom of it if you like," he said, "I won't be working here anymore." He walked out abruptly.

This upset Chelsea. The people who worked under her were like her family. The fact that one had decided not to be part of the family anymore, for spurious reasons was a hard pill to swallow. On top of that he'd said he got the information from Oliver Stancroft, and it was more than could be handled. She was furious. She used her lunch break that day to drive over to the Stancroft bank.

She marched right into Oliver Stancroft's office and sat down.

"You've got a lot of nerve coming in here," he said.

"I've got a lot nerve? I do?" Chelsea protested.

"That's right. You goddamn Tollivers planning to come in here and steal our trade secrets again?"

"You work in a bank, Oliver. There aren't any damn trade secrets."

"Oh you've got a lot of nerve," he repeated. He had no other retort.

"What have you been telling my employees?" Chelsea asked.

"The truth!"

"Evidently not, because Lyle Hoover left my company today due to information he got from you. He thinks I'm up to my elbows in shady underhanded dealings."

"Well aren't you?"

"No!" she shouted, "We make clothes. Nothing underhanded."

Oliver stood up, leaned in, and spoke with a slow, low gravelly tone, "Where's my coffee mug?" he asked. He folded his arms conclusively as if to say "check and mate."

"Your....what?"

"You know exactly what I'm talking about Tolliver," he said with as much sneer as he could put on her last name.

"You have a coffee mug sitting right there," she said gesturing. It was true, there was a mug sitting on his desk from the morning.

"Not this mug," she snarled, "Nixon's mug."

"Nixon?" she said, trying not to laugh.

"What's so funny?" he snapped.

"A number of things," she said, "starting with Nixon is dead."

"I know he's dead, you...." he didn't find an insult to finish the sentence with. "I have his mug. A mug he used when he was alive."

"And you think I know where it is?"

"Yes..." the absurdity of this was allowing Oliver his very first peek at it.

"And that's why Lyle Hoover quit his job today. Because you think I stole some coffee mug Nixon used?"

His brain slipped a gear trying to respond to this. Somehow this conversation had gotten away from him, he felt.

He found the right angle and pressed again, "No, because you're working to undermine me through the mug. It's not just that it's gone."

"I have nothing to do with your stupid coffee mug!" she shouted.

"So you say," Oliver replied.

"This is preposterous," Chelsea said, getting up to leave.

"You can't leave now," he protested.

"I'm wasting my time," she said and left.

Oliver sat back down. Adrenaline was still pumping through him. His hands were shaking. He was aware of himself enough to know not to do anything until he'd calmed down. So he just sat and stared at picture of his wife and kids that was on his desk.

He heard a knock at his office door and looked up. Still breathing hard. Still shaking. It was David Thompson.

"Oliver, your wife is here."

"Timing isn't good," he said, "What does she need?"

Beverly stepped around David into the room. She was holding the Nixon mug, "Thank you, David," she said and shut the door to the office behind her.

"You had it this whole time?" Oliver said.

She sighed and rolled her eyes, "No. No one is out to get you. You had it this whole time."

"I did?"

"Yes it was in your photography studio."

"My...OHHH!" he remembered taking the photos of the mug in the room off the garage. He hadn't looked there.

"Now, what do you have to say for yourself?"

"I...I'm sorry. I've made a total ass of myself."

"You have."

"I just hope that Chelsea Tolliver doesn't find out where it was this whole time."

"I just saw her in the parking lot and told her all about it. She already knows. What did you say to that woman?"

"I...well...."

The next day at Alice's Diner, Lyle Hoover recounted time everyone how Oliver Stancroft had stolen his own coffee mug.

"But how do *you* know?" one of them asked, "He wouldn't talk about it yesterday."

"Chelsea Tolliver explained the whole thing to me last night. She came to my house to ask me to take my old job back."

"Did you say yes? Do you think you can trust her?"

"Yes, I think I can."

The Miles Coontz Murders

Harry's old sedan growled irritably outside Marvin's house. Marvin walked up to the car and leaned on through the passenger window, "Hey Harry! How are you?"

"Get in. We got a tip we have to check out," said Harry.

Marvin swung open the passenger side door and lowered himself into Harry's car. The seats were sun faded from a red fabric to a pale pink color. Harry used to smoke in his car, you could still smell it hanging around in the air. There was even a crumpled empty cigarette pack sticking out from under the floor mat by Marvin's toes. The air was full of an oppressive stale deadness.

There were little scraps of paper with notes on them: names and phone numbers mostly.

"I hope I wasn't interrupting anything important," Harry said.

"Eh, not really," Marvin said, "I was reading this article on how to prepare for an interview. How your resume should look, what you should wear, what kinds of things you should and shouldn't talk about. Did you know it's considered rude to ask about pay in your interview?"

"Hmm," said Harry, "I think I did."

"News to me. I can pass that article along to you if you want. Maybe you could put it to good use."

"I would appreciate that."

"Anyway, what's this tip all about?" asked Marvin.

"Someone called me and said Miles Coontz is in the area, " said Harry.

"Miles Coontz, the cop-killer? You get a little obsessed with him. Is he your white whale?"

"That Miles Coontz. Detective killer actually. He seems to target guys like you and me. But this time we got the upper hand. This time wc're gonna get him."

"Right on," said Marvin.

"I'd appreciate it if you didn't use words like obsessed. They suggest I'm irrational. This guy has a history with the department. We'd all like to see him brought in. It's not obsessed. It's our job.

"Years back, there was a detective who was murdered when I was on patrol, he was one of these young ambitious guys headed for promotion just like you. Then he was dead.

"He was called out to this place on the way to Vicksburg because of some kind of tip or other. He never told anyone what it was, and nobody ever heard from him again to ask. They found his body in a field with a bullet wound consistent with a Luger.

"Our prime suspect was this vagrant Coontz who seemed to have a vendetta against cops. Mostly because we'd ruled everything else out. There was nobody else it could have been. Coontz had blown into Clapford County somehow and vanished somehow without anyone knowing where he came from, where he went, how he moved around. Nothing.

"Several years after that when Coontz was back in town, same thing: another promising detective gets called out on some kind of something. Nobody knows what, and that detective was never heard from again.

"This time they found his body out towards Valico. Same bullet wound type, consistent with a Luger. It sure seemed to be the same shooter."

"And he got off?"

"We never had enough to hold him, and even if we had, we never could find him. He was a ghost. It was like he was never even there."

"So you've never seen him?"

"Practically nobody has, at least nobody that's alive."

"So how do you know he's in town?"

"I got a call. Anonymous tip. He's at the old Turkelson Mine. Past the miner's quarters in the very back."

"You think it's really him?"

"I guess we won't know until we find him."

Marvin thought about this for a second, "What if this tip ain't legit?"

"Well we go home I guess, and write a sad song about it. Why would anyone be making this kind of thing up?"

"To lure two cops out into the middle of nowhere."

Harry just grunted. A pensive quiet fell over the pair for a moment, "He's never done two cops," Harry said, "We got the upper hand this time."

"Did you call dispatch and let them know where we were headed?" asked Marvin.

"Oh geez, I forgot to mention: I was trying to do that just before I got to your house and it wouldn't go through."

"Its protocol you know."

"Yeah yeah yeah, I know. Call it in before we get there, will ya?"

"Dispatch this is Mason, " Marvin said into the radio, "Dispatch, come in."

The radio hissed. No one was heard.

"Dispatch this is Mason..."

Static.

"We might be in a dead spot, " said Harry, "Should we turn back?"

"Nah, we're practically there already, " said Marvin, "Drive on. We can let them know where we were when we bring him in."

"Right on, " said Harry.

The mine itself was decades old. It had been discovered in 1940 by a man called Patrick Turkelson, who began exploiting it immediately in the service of his country during the Second World War, but more importantly in the service of his wallet whilst demand was high. Inside the mine, rooms were carved out of the rock and used to house miners, to hold provisions, cook meals, and live a whole underground life. Outside the mine a small village called Steamsburg sprang up to house miners, their families, and provide a place to go drink on the weekends.

The mine wasn't deep, it turned out, it was just wide. The miners quickly exhausted it within a few years, and it stood abandoned after that. Steamsburg withered away to what it is today: largely abandoned, populated only by the disastrously poor. Turkelson Manor, "the house that coal built" still stands half completed. Construction stopped when the mine ran out. The incomplete structure still stands there gloomily decaying in mid-creation, reminding passers by that in this little corner of the world, ambition doesn't pay.

The mouth of the mine was set into the side of a hill back in the woods west of the little village. There was a field outside of it that had been graveled at some point to serve as a parking lot and loading zone. That field was now fenced in and kept locked up. The police were called frequently to evict someone who had broken in, despite the entire area being decorated with bright yellow signs warning against trespassing and the dangers of exploring an abandoned coal mine. Nevertheless there was a certain appeal to a forgotten hole in the ground secured from the world by a fence and hidden from view by forest, particularly for drug users and teenage lovers.

The lock was broken and the gate was ajar when Harry and Marvin pulled up. There was really nothing unusual in that. The old parking lot was empty. Harry pulled to a stop near the mouth of the mine and shut the car off.

It took Marvin and Harry a full thirty minutes to walk from the car parked at the entrance all the way to the back rooms of the mine where the caller had said Miles Coontz would be.

The tip was helpful because if they hadn't had a lead, a place to start, searching all of the rooms in the mine could take days. Harry walked behind Marvin. He let him search all over with his flashlight clearing each section before moving on toward the miners quarters at the back of the mine.

Dust hung everywhere in the air and seemed to be suspended there, unchanged by the passing of time. It seemed to Marvin that dust kicked up by the miners during the war was still lingering in flight.

They moved methodically, carefully, room by room, back the main corridor through the mine. There were no signs of life anywhere. Only the echoes of their footsteps, and the echoes of their breaths.

After a bit, Marvin whispered, "You must have seen all kind of cops in your years."

"Say what?" asked Harry.

"You've been on the force a long time. You must have seen a lot of cops come and go."

"I reckon."

"What's the secret?"

"Huh?"

"Folks move up, right? Get promoted, move up the ranks... How do they do it?"

"I don't know. Whatever it is, it sure ain't asking an old-timer who's been passed up for every special assignment, promotion or transfer that comes along. If I knew the secret I'd be out of here! What a dumb question kid."

"I'm sorry."

"Just don't ask the audience how the magician did the trick."

"All right, all right. I hear you."

"Good. Shut up now. If he hears us and gets spooked we'll never find him in here."

Along the way there were many false alarms. Marvin would catch sight of some artifact or another that merited closer inspection. They found syringes, condom wrappers, beer cans, cigarette butts, even a forgotten styrofoam cooler that now held only water. Anything anyone wanted to keep hidden had taken place back in the dusty dark of the mine. Harry thought of all the depravity the mine had seen against its will and shuddered, offering a silent apology to the rock.

At long last, they reached the quarters. Wooden bunk frames stretched back six deep and two across to the far wall. It was immediately evident no one had been here in some time.

"He's not here, " said Marvin turning slowly around with the flashlight.

He came to rest on Harry. Harry had a gun drawn and was aiming it at Marvin.

"He is here, Marvin. He's right here looking at you."

"What are you doing, Harry?"

"Throw your gun on the floor."

"What?"

"Do it!" he snarled.

Marvin did it.

"You want to know the secret? How to move up?" Harry asked, "It's 'Be young and handsome. Have polish.' That's it, so long as you have some idea what you're doing. It's not be good at your job. It's not solve more cases. It's not even suck up to the boss. I'm tired of it. I've outperformed each of the last five detectives chosen over me for promotions. And I'm kicking your tail too on metrics by the way, but they'll pick you. I'm too old, they think. I'm a liability."

"Well..."

"Shut up! This ain't your time to speak.

"The first time was fifteen years ago. My partner got picked over me for promotion. It didn't make sense. I was angry. We came out here on some made up reason and I took care of him. Because I was angry, you see? And I thought with him out of the way I was guaranteed to get it. Nope! Emotionally compromised. Department shrink said I needed some time off. They gave the job to some other guy from Vicksburg. I didn't even try to get the Miles Coontz story off the ground. Someone just made it up that the murderer must have been some old homeless guy who'd just left town. He wouldn't have hurt a fly, but we were pinning murder on him. That was fine with me.

"Then about eight years ago, the same thing. My partner is the department darling. No promotion yet, but it's coming. You can smell it, you know. Back to the Turkelson Mine we came. Looking for Miles Coontz, I told him. Just like I told you. Different room that time. That's the beauty of this place. There are ninety rooms in this mine. You can pick and choose if you want to.

"He never showed up to work again, and I paid some other vagrant to say he'd been traveling with Miles Coontz. People didn't bother to check too hard. They were already telling themselves the story of what 'really' happened.

"And now there's you..."

"You won't get away with this..."

"Miles will. He always does. Everyone knows Miles did it, and nobody will ever stop him."

"You're insane."

"Nah, just sick of young turds like you getting whatever you want."

"But I don't I-"

The gunshot was deafening inside the room.

Harry started back immediately without another look. It was a long way to walk alone.

GLUE on Campus

In my office in the philosophy department wing of the fine arts building I have a small window to the outside world. It is skinny and not very tall. Through it, when I remember it's there and choose to lean over and look through it, I can see the campus courtyard where new student orientations, student protests, carnival fundraisers, and a dozen other regular activities happen.

When the courtyard isn't scheduled with an event, it remains generally busy. When people could still smoke on campus, it used to be even busier. Every now and then I see Pythagoras out there flailing his arms around and jumping up and down. "Dancing," he calls it. When I see Pythagoras, I sigh. I know it means I'm being paid a visit by the boys: Albert Einstein, Johannes Kepler, and Pythagoras. They come to my office, set up some board game on my table, and fritter away time.

When this began I imagined I was selected by some celestial being to have the brilliant minds of the ages visit me and impart the wisdom they had accumulated over the years to me. You can imagine how it disabuses one of such a notion to have Albert Einstein explain to you, from beyond the grave, that he's more interested in beating you in Chutes and Ladders than telling you the secrets of the universe.

"It's all we do all day long," said Kepler, "Answer questions about what we think of the cosmos."

"Questions from who?" I asked.

"The tourists!" Pythagoras explained.

"Tourists? You have visitors up there...wherever you are?"

"This is what we call the new arrivals," said Einstein, "They're all so awestruck for the first couple of weeks. They go around gawking and oohing and ahh-ing for a while and then they get bored."

"They get bored?"

"Well sure, everything's amazing and nothing isn't," said Pythagoras, "There is no variety. The Great Beyond is a real snooze fest after a while."

"That's why we come to see you," said Kepler, "To get a break."

"Oh that makes a fella feel great," I said, "You visit me to get away from amazing people."

"Well..." said Einstein, trailing off.

I came to the realization pretty quickly that the boys weren't real. They were figments if my imagination, and I was loonier than a Canadian dollar.

I, Dr. James Wilson, am not of sound mind.

The problem with GLUE started a few weeks after the Fall semester started. The Generous Light of the Universe and Earth was a cult that started in Hardy in the 1960s, and had spread to satellite campuses all over the world. The headquarters of the organization were in Clapford County in the woods on a heavily guarded compound complete with razor wire and men and women with assault rifles. It was a concern for the locals.

Once a year or so, GLUE showed up on the campus of Hardy Community College to recruit lost sheep, so to speak, and shepherd them back to their compound. These recruits were rarely heard from again, and this was troubling enough in itself.

This particular visit however, happened to follow mere weeks after an ugly incident in El Paso, Texas that was widely reported to have been connected to GLUE.

The particulars of *that* incident were that a certain local politician had made exposing GLUE to the world her pet project. She was, like much of the faculty here, concerned about young impressionable minds being duped into joining a mystery organization never to be heard from again. She made statements in local newspapers, on television, and the story had even been picked up by a few national outlets.

One day, she and her husband and two adult sons were in their car on their way to a gun range, hauling enough artillery to arm a small militia. Then, something, no one is quite sure what, happened. All four in the car were murdered by someone who left absolutely no trace, and must have acted with vicious speed. Not one of the guns in the car was used. Not even the one in glove compartment.

They didn't even have time to open the glove compartment.

A number of theories and conjectures began to circle around the story. Many of which pointed the blame at The Generous Light of the Universe and Earth. A group here in Hardy tried to have the cult removed, but there was no ground to stand on. There was only the flimsiest of provable connections to the case in Texas. Aside from being creepy and cultish, GLUE were model citizens of the county. They paid taxes on time and voted.

The bar is pretty low for model citizens these days.

There was even a petition to ban them from coming to the college. This was dismissed as censorship, and the recruitment drive was allowed to proceed as normal. However, a protest was formed for students and community members to voice their concerns on the other side of the courtyard. Ideas were exchanged, though neither side took any in from the other.

After this, the problems began. GLUE were embarrassed by this incident on their home soil. They returned to campus every day after that to counter protest. They brought with them a dozen or so men and women with assault rifles for protection.

This seemed like overkill to the students, whose passion for free speech was suddenly inflamed. Two entrenched sides formed in the courtyard every day in a long futile stalemate.

I told Einstein and the boys from the Great Beyond about it. Pythagoras laughed that wild loud laugh of his and offered no substantive comment. Kepler just stared at me for a long beat and said, "We know."

"The thing is though, it's really ruined everything here. Morale is down. Attendance is down. The courtyard is a war zone. No one knows what to do."

"We know," said Kepler.

"You can't get involved," said Einstein shuffling a deck of cards, "not directly anyway. You're a professor of this fine institution. Maybe you can help guide your students to a solution."

"That's brilliant," I said.

"We know," said Kepler.

"How does everyone feel about canasta?" Einstein asked.

Pythagoras laughed and laughed.

There was a student I had, Martha Felson, who looked on me as something of a mentor. I don't know why. She was wild about Kierkegaard and I was unwilling to make any leaps of faith. I would hurl Wittgenstein at her. The old "the world is made of facts" and "what we cannot speak about we must pass over in silence" got nowhere with her. But it was a doomed discussion before it even started, I suppose.

Martha was very involved in the protests against GLUE. It seemed to me if I had any capacity to influence the student side, it was through Martha and my ill-fated mentorship of being un-listened-to.

I invited her to my office for consultation. Einstein, Pythagoras and Kepler followed her in.

Martha was an outside-the-herd sort of person. Most philosophy students are. Her version of otherness was as thoroughgoing as I have seen. She dressed with no discernible style, theme, or objective. She seemed to be wearing clothes that were selected arbitrarily. Sometimes they fit, sometimes they did not. She came into my office wearing blue jeans that were far too wide for her and a bit too short. She had them cinched tight at the waist with a belt. She was wearing one of the welcome shirts they give out the first week of the semester. Her shoes did not match.

I need to repeat that.

She was wearing two different shoes.

"You wanted to see me, Dr. Wilson?"

"How do you do?" I said. Pythagoras laughed at me.

"Uhh, I'm fine," she said, "How are you?"

"Yeah," she said, "good. I got this Kant class this semester. I kind of hate it."

"Ah well..." said Einstein. I glared at him.

"I see you've been involved in these protests."

"Oh those people rent their land from my family. I don't know if anyone knows that or not, but I'd rather they didn't find out. Especially after what happened in Texas. They deserve to be protested. It's in line with my communal ideals."

"Sure. Right. I just wonder what the objective is. Is that it to stay consistent with your ideals?"

"Well yeah. I mean, we want them to leave. Stop coming here."

"And you're doing that by giving them attention?"

"What?"

"They're here counter protesting the students. This is one of those scenarios where maybe the right thing to do is what doesn't feel like the right thing to do. You want them to leave so you're protesting, but your protesting is the reason they're staying. They're getting press. You're doing them a favor.

"The alternative is not protesting, which feels like you're sending a message of acceptance. 'We're okay with you guys and your whatever you do.' But it isn't. It's the way to win. You get them to leave. They lose the attention so there's no reason to stay. Everyone goes back to normal college life at Hardy."

"This sounds consequentialist," she said. I turned away from her and wiped a tear from my eye. I was so proud. I couldn't remember if I taught her in Ethics or not, but it didn't matter. It was one of my favorite words to hear a student say.

"Well sure," I managed.

"I don't think Kant would approve."

"He wouldn't," Kepler said. I glanced at him. I must admit, the thought of irritating Kant brought me some joy.

"Anyway," Martha continued, "we're not backing down from them. If anyone is giving up it's them."

"I'm not suggesting giving up. I'm suggesting a strategy to get them to leave."

"And the students are bonding, and becoming stronger: energized, mobilized...awakened, I guess."

"Just give it some consideration."

"I can do that, Dr. Wilson."

Weeks went by with little visible change. Either Martha had decided against following my advice, or she had proposed the idea to the other students and no one had listened to her.

As September started to turn its attention to hanging up its hat and letting October have a turn, a new group began showing up on campus. The local gun rights activists started showing up. This situation had nothing to do with gun rights, of course, but that rarely impedes the average gun rights activist. He merely scours the scene for some tangential connection to his pet issue, or interprets the scenario as a metaphor for his pet issue, or invents some other reason entirely divorced from reality.

In our unhappy case, the gun rights people saw students protesting people who were carrying guns, and that was enough for them to show up and defend GLUE against being silenced in this particular courtyard.

Under normal circumstances their exaggeratedly large guns would have escalated the arms level in the courtyard of the college, but GLUE had the gun rights folks out-gunned by a considerable margin.

For their part, GLUE looked on the new presence as adversaries. They were armed outsiders showing up in protest. The cult took aim at the gun folks, and a whole new standoff developed. The students taking issue with the gun folks as much as they took issue with GLUE, the gun folks taking issue with the students and feeling betrayed by GLUE, and GLUE feeling threatened by everything.

Then the National Guard showed up to keep the peace, which only amplified the tension. The whole place was a matchbook soaked in gasoline waiting for a spark.

I could tell you it was unpleasant being on campus around this time. Obviously that's underselling it quite a bit. Everyone was on edge, and nobody wanted to talk about it. Students stopped coming to classes. I had mixed feelings about this. I wanted them to be in class and learn and succeed, but I wanted them to be safe doing it.

My colleagues started to worry about their jobs. A professor who was especially adept at stirring up fear wondered what would happen to us all if people heard about this and no one ever wanted to come to our little school again.

I was worried. You can tell when I'm agitated because I see more of the Boys when I've got a lot on my mind. They normally come by once a week or so. During this they were stopping by two to three times a day.

"You guys are getting a lot more breaks lately," I said.

"It's slow up there," said Kepler.

"Also they want a firsthand account of what's going on down here," said Einstein.

"We're field reporters," said Pythagoras.

"The student," Einstein said, "why hasn't she stopped this?"

"Martha?" I asked.

I hadn't noticed but she was standing in the door of my office. I was looking away from her.

"Of course Martha. You gave her a plan. Why hasn't she acted on it?" he said.

"I don't know. Maybe she tried."

"Someone has to do something," Kepler chimed in.

"Want me to go talk to them?" Pythagoras asked.

"By all means go and give us some peace from your eternal idiocy," said Einstein.

We watched through my little office window as a figment of my imagination tried to talk sense into people who couldn't see or hear him. During this time I suppose Martha was just standing behind me wondering what on earth I was doing. I wouldn't have been able to explain anyway.

"Why can't I fix this?" I asked Einstein.

"You have to preserve a neutral position while you're here. Students can speak their mind, employees can't. Maybe they should, but they can't. You need your Martha to come through."

"I'm sure she'll do the right thing," I said.

"Dr. Wilson?" Martha said. That found me off my guard. I felt like I'd been caught in the middle of something truly embarrassing. I guess in a manner of speaking I was. Although it is frequently passed around in rumor on campus that I am bananas, cuckoo, nutty, cracked up, bonkers, etc., you can never be too sure who has heard that and who has not.

"Martha! I wasn't expecting you," I said, turning around.

"What were you doing?"

"Eh? Oh, nothing. Talking to myself mostly," I gave Kepler and Einstein a glance, "That and taking in the scene in the courtyard."

"It's gotten worse," she said.

"Yes, that it has."

"I don't know what to do."

"Well, I think the same advice still applies, take the student protest out of the equation. Everything de-escalates after that."

"I understand that," she said, "but the students are opposed. They don't want it to look like we were scared off. Then that opens the gate to who-knows-what after them."

"Ahh, the 'running scared' story is the narrative the spectators will create for themselves, unless you give them a different one first."

"What?"

"Go everywhere else: the papers, the radio, television whoever will listen to you. Tell them the protest has power because the students gave it power, and the students have the power to silence it.

"Then wait a week and silence it."

She thought about it for a minute, "I don't think that's strong enough."

"I don't either, but it's better than what we've got."

Kepler shrugged.

"I wish there was a way to send a message to them not to ever come back," she said.

Einstein raised his finger as if he had an idea. "There might be a way. Talk with the students, and if they're agreeable, start laying the foundation for controlling your story. Then come back and see me. We might have a better plan by then," this all started to look hopeful to me. I was getting energized in my own plan. I saw it all playing out clearly and effortlessly. I was excited.

"I guess I can talk to them again," Martha said, definitely less energized than I was.

She left the room pensive and despondent. Einstein sprang up from his chair and began speaking, "How do you get rid of them? How do you make sure they never come back? You've got to hit them where it matters to them. They've got attention right now, sure. That draws sympathy to their cause, sure. But what did they want to stop from coming out in Texas? That politician knew something. They were afraid of it, whatever it was. It's leverage against them. Tell them it's coming out if they don't leave, and if they leave and never come back it never sees the light of day. Problem solved," he rubbed his hands together in a pantomime of cleaning the chalk from them.

"We don't know what it was she knew," I said.

"We find out," he said.

"And they kill you," said Kepler, "I'm fine with this. We can find someone else to visit on break, but you, you might not want this to happen?"

"Yeah, and they kill us if we have that information," I said echoing Kepler, "Besides you say we find out as if that were simple to do. This lady in Texas spent a long time on this. She had resources and informants. We have nothing."

"Then what do you suggest?" Einstein said.

"I don't know," I shrugged.

"Well it's easy to criticize isn't it? But when it's your turn to contribute you don't have anything."

Just the Pythagoras came back in panting, "They're crazy. We need to figure out a way to get rid of them!"

"We know!" said Kepler.

The four of us quieted down and had a good long ponder about it.

Martha came back into my office the next day a changed person, she seemed buoyant, bouncy even. It made me uncomfortable, "Martha I don't have a good strong plan for you. We had a good long ponder about it, but nothing."

"We?" she asked.

"Well um, you know."

She stared at me blankly.

"I guess you don't know."

"No..."

"Well I suppose it's neither here not there. I don't have any plan for you, I didn't come up with anything."

"Oh that's okay. I did."

"You did? That's a shame. I could have saved my ponder. What is your plan?"

"You'll see."

"Hmmm, okay," I said, a little disappointed, "You came here to tell me you have a plan but not what it is?"

"Oh no I came here to tell you we were on the news this morning."

"Oh interesting," is all I could manage.

"We're following your plan, too. We told the world we were going to bring this thing to a close. They may still say we ran away, but I suppose someone will always say that no matter what."

"That's true. I'm glad you are finally putting a stop to this. When is it happening?"

"Today," she said.

True to her word, that day the student protest almost completely broke up all at once in an apparently choreographed maneuver. Only Martha was left in their section of the courtyard. The other factions were very confused by this development, but seemed to be celebrating their accomplishment, as if that last chant of god-knows-what they were chanting was the one that did the trick. At least this is how it looked from where I sat with my face pressed against my tiny office window.

Then I watched with some horror as Martha walked directly up to the GLUE group. A couple of the cult members walked up to her, and there was a brief parlay in the courtyard.

"Fascinating," said Kepler. Oh great, I thought, my friends are here.

"What is she doing?" Einstein asked.

"Her plan," I said.

The parlay broke up, Martha turned around and walked straight out of the courtyard. Her part was done.

The cult members huddled and discussed what had passed in the parlay, and then made nearly as choreographed an exit as the students had made.

"It's ending!" yelled Pythagoras and then he started jumping and screaming. Typical day for Pythagoras.

This left only the gun rights folks and the national guard in the courtyard. No one had communicated anything with those groups, and they looked like they weren't sure what was happening. At first a few gun people left, and then the group started to fragment and dissipate. One of them seemed determined to stay no matter what. He folded his arms and set his stance wide. He held that position all the way up until there were only two men left in that group. When his buddy threw in the towel, he shrugged and followed him out. The national guard held its position for a few beats after the courtyard emptied. Then someone radioed in an order. We could see a guy talking on his radio. After that they were gone too.

The entire campus relaxed palpably. Students were seen back in classes later that day, and taking selfies in the courtyard that same afternoon. My colleagues returned to walking around the office and I did not see my imaginary friends from the Great Beyond for an entire week.

With our world settling back into its normal routine, I got busy returning to teaching classes and having folks take advantage of office hours and didn't have a chance to catch up with Martha for a few weeks.

When I saw her again she was walking the opposite direction from me in the hall outside my office.

"Dr. Wilson!" she said, "You are just who I was coming to see."

"I'm glad to see you," I said.

"I haven't seen you since the showdown in the courtyard."

"Oh right," I said absently. I was good at pretending to forget things.

"GLUE has agreed never to come back to our campus again."

"Oh really? That's marvelous," I said.

"Aren't you going to ask me why?"

"Why what?" I said. Again, excellent pretender.

"Why they're not coming back."

"Oh I suppose I was getting curious about that," I said, "What did you say to them that day to get them to go away?"

"I told them my name."

"Your name?"

"Yep. My family owns the land they rent. They didn't want to jeopardize their compound."

"And that's why they're never coming back?"

"No. That's why they left that day. They're never coming back because I struck a deal with them: agree to never come back and I'll become their spokesperson and fix their public image."

"Fix? What about your communal ideals?"

"This is how I serve them."

"I am very confused by this," I said.

"By doing this job, I keep this cult from appearing on our campus."

"Yes but you make them look better in the eyes of the public. You grow their influence. They recruit more young people and it causes even more harm in the long run."

"I don't think any more people will actually join. I think there are only so many people they can fool at a given time. So their numbers will be about the same. No harm no foul, but we gain by keeping them off our campus."

"But what if you accidentally improve their numbers?" I said.

"I don't think I will," she said, "But being on the inside I do have some control over how that goes."

"Are you sure about this?" I asked.

"It's for the best," she said, "I thought you'd be proud I was being a good consequentialist."

I sighed at her, "Good luck."

"Thanks Dr. Wilson."

From inside my office, Pythagoras cackled.

Clapford Printing

Bill Stegner went to Clapford middle and high schools as consciously as someone breathes air: unthinkingly, instinctively. His performance was somewhat uninspired. It had never occurred to him that excelling at school was even an option. School was just something that happened to him for a while, and then it was over, like a storm to be weathered. Maybe you could do a better job at handling the storm, but the important bit was enduring it, as far as Bill could tell.

That was something he thought a lot about later in life. Why didn't anyone tell me how much I stood to lose by not taking it more seriously? Upon reflection, he realized he had been told—daily—by teachers, administrators, neighbors, parents, aunts, uncles, cousins, clergy, and postal workers. Somehow the meaning of what they'd told him didn't seem to be present in the content of what he remembered them saying. It was all consigned to the same general voice that said not to put his elbows on the table, or to say "please" and "thank you": the sorts of things a young man only takes seriously when someone else is looking.

Ah well, he mused, when my children are that age, I'll make sure they know what I wish I'd known. It was precisely the same thought his father had when thinking about raising Bill.

Bill worked for Bella Clapford, county royalty and former classmate. Bella was heir to the county namesake's fortune and lucrative printing business. Clapford Printing was responsible for the brochures going around practically every doctor's office in the country warning about the dangers of this or that activity.

They also printed about half of the Midwest's wedding invitations.

Bill was responsible for Quality Assurance at Clapford. Machine operators would bring him samples from their orders when they'd gotten them ready for printing. He checked to make sure type wasn't crooked, colors were correct, and there were no typos. If he was satisfied, he gave them approval to run the order.

He was happy enough to be out of a production job, but he wasn't quite out of the factory yet, and the secretaries, account reps, and managers across the street in the offices seemed to Bill to lead such luxurious lives by comparison. For one thing, it was a lot quieter over there.

And then there was Bella Clapford. Bill had nurtured a crush on Bella since their early days in Clapford Middle School.

Back then it was tacitly agreed upon by God and everyone that, due to her family wealth and social position, Bella was off-limits to ordinary townsfolk. Everyone stayed away. Bill admired her from afar, but tried to stay in her general vicinity. It was how he came to be at the printing company.

A little more effort back in school, Bill reckoned, and I could at least be over in the same building as her, instead of across the street in this factory. When Bella stopped by the factory, she'd cut it short. It's too noisy for small talk. Only necessities would be exchanged. But over there, I'm sure it's quiet. There's time for idle chitchat, he mused.

"Can you give me an approval on this order, Bill?" Wayne Curtis laid out a bright brochure about the dangers of second-hand smoke to children.

"Wayne, what did you want to be when you grew up?" Bill asked wistfully.

"Bill, I wanted to be done with this order. Can you take a look?"

"You're running downhill," he pointed to the type that was out of parallel with the edge of the sheet, "Straighten it up and bring it back here."

Wayne sighed an exaggerated sigh, picked up his sheets, and left the room.

Bill took a legal pad out of his desk and wrote at the top of the page "JOBS I WOULD BE GOOD AT," then leaned back and stared at the wall. He wrote nothing beneath it. He noticed Bella Clapford was on the factory floor.

Bella was the de facto owner of the company. Her father was still around as the on-paper owner: a figurehead she could put in front of any old-fashioned bigots who thought a woman couldn't do the job she was already doing. He owned the company, but it was hers to run and inherit. She had every intention of building the business, finding every efficiency, improving every process and--once it was legally hers--selling it to the highest bidder.

Bella's real passion was for the stage. In her mind, she was an actress just waiting for her time to go set the world on fire. For her time to come, though, she had to clear the responsibility of the company from her conscience. That meant either hiring someone else to run it or selling it. And since it didn't make enough money to add executive staff, a sale was the only solution. There were even offers on the table to choose from when the time came.

In the meantime, increasing the asking price was her sole aim in life, and she was extremely adept at reducing costs, increasing revenue, and inspiring productivity. These regular visits to the floor seemed aimless to the workers, but they were extremely strategic.

As a student, Bella had been generally skilled without applying herself too much. She was one of those rare pupils who seem to have an intuitive understanding of everything without really mastering anything.

She had only the vaguest notion that no one really talked to her. People spoke to her, of course, but the conversations were of the shallowest nature possible. She had friends, but none dared to get too close.

Her friends all dated, and had serious boyfriends. She spent many nights crying quietly into her pillow over the fact that none seemed capable of being in love with Bella Clapford.

Her parents leveraged some contacts to enroll Bella into a private college in Ohio, there she had studied business as she was told to do, but minored in theater, explaining to her father that it could only aid in presentations to clients when securing new business for the company.

As an actor, she was merely passable. Her chief accomplishment was a supporting role in the campus's production of *Antigone*. This show was so sparsely attended it was not even reviewed in the school paper. Had the review ran, Bella would have given up on acting entirely.

After college she returned home to Clapford County where a junior account representative position awaited her at her father's company. Periodically, he would promote her until she reached the rank of Senior Vice President and de facto owner.

But now she was walking the factory floor, pretending to have no aim whatsoever. Bill Stegner had no work at the moment, and Wayne's brochure was the only thing close to ready for QA to review. So he left his work area and walked over to Wayne's machine. This way he could appear busy as well as put himself in Bella's path.

"Come to check on me?" Wayne asked.

"No, I just don't have anything else to do, and the boss lady's walking around."

"Ah well, I was just headed back to you. It's ready." The two men leaned over the sheets to review them and did not see Bella Clapford walk up to his desk and pick up a legal pad.

Bill approved the job and turned around. He saw Bella standing at his desk. He went straight back over to her.

"Tell me about this," she said, sliding the legal pad in front of Bill.

He was dumbstruck. "I-umm-I-wanted a-umm..."

"What? You wanted a what?"

"I thought that --- umm --- what if I --- umm --- worked from the office?" he was pleased that he'd gotten the main thrust of his idea out there: he wanted a job across the street.

"That would make the press operators have to cross the street to get their order QA'd. Right now it's a 30 second commute for them. You're adding in minutes per order. It adds up."

That wasn't what he meant, but a frantic, chaotic determination set itself up in Bill's mind. This new idea suddenly became all encompassing. It blurred out his sense of protocol and manners, and he was going to take a chance on it, "Let someone else do QA. I'm worth more than that to the company. I can do something else."

Bella saw a new species of Bill Stegner, and she took a second to observe this new creature's attributes. This Bill was reckless, bold, and apparently unhappy with his working conditions. Unhappy workers breed more unhappy workers. However, just because someone wants a new position it doesn't mean they get one. That would be chaos.

"There's nothing on this list, Bill. What jobs would you be good at?"

Bill's heart sank. He read an indictment of his entire career in her question. What jobs would I be good at? I can't even fill out a list! "I guess...I guess I don't know. I need to learn more about them."

The more familiar breed of Bill Stegner stood in front of her. He was no longer reckless and bold. He was a timid self-doubting duck, "What about this, Bill: I'll write down five I think you can do, and you write down five you think you can do. If we both have the same job on our lists, we'll set up a job shadow for you, and you can see what you think."

Bill was over the moon, "Thank you Bella!"

"Thank you Bill."

Bill was beside himself for the rest of the day. He made a list of all the jobs he knew about from across the street, and carefully considered each one. He crossed off ones he knew he couldn't do or thought were a demotion.

He went home that evening and paced up and down his drab living room. Bella Clapford is thinking about me, he thought. Implanting this thought was the genius of Bella's strategy.

He imagined her sitting at a desk, what kind of desk does Bella Clapford have in her home? A giant oak desk, perhaps, with cherubs carved into to legs. There she sits with her own legal pad, thinking -- no, *concentrating*-- on Bill Stegner. I'm sure she sees potential in me that I don't see in myself. It's probably hard for her to narrow her list down to five. Excitement kept building in Bill as he paced back and forth.

Then, there was a knock on the door. Bill's reverie evaporated. He lived in what the locals called a Print-Mold house. They were called this because to house all the print factory workers, a construction company had built a square subdivision with street after street of houses, all with exactly the same design and floor plan, as if they were all from the same mold. There were no customizations. The work was quick and cheap.

Bill's print-mold house was in the back of the square neighborhood. No one would just pick his house out at random. A stranger knocking on his door meant someone going door to door: mormons, politicians, Girl Scouts.

He opened the door in mild annoyance, and there stood Bella Clapford. Immediately his annoyance turned to embarrassment. She had come to his lowly hovel. This house was not up to the task of welcoming her.

"Hello, Bella?" he said nervously, "What brings you here?"

"You're lost," she said.

"I'm at home. I'm beginning to think you are the one who is lost."

"You don't know how to move forward in your career," she said, "I thought about your empty notepad all evening. You want to go somewhere but you don't know where. You don't know how to get there. You don't even really know where you are now. You're lost."

"Is this what you came here to tell me?" Bill asked, "Because I think we could have talked tomorrow..."

"I do apologize. I shouldn't have bothered you at home," she said, acknowledging the faux pas she'd committed without seeming to care too much that she'd committed it, "I just couldn't set it aside. It would have driven me crazy."

"Oh I see," Bill said, unsure of what to say, "Don't worry about it."

"Is this your place? May I come in?" Bella asked.

"It's nothing special..." he hesitated, "but of course. Come in."

Bill stepped to the side and let her enter. He looked around at his tiny living room with fresh eyes. It looked ridiculous to him suddenly, like a child's imitation of what a grown up would have.

"This is lovely," said Bella.

"Honestly?" asked Bill.

"Sure!" Bella beamed.

"So I'm lost..." Bill said.

"We're both lost," she said.

"I don't follow..."

"I'm not where I'm supposed to be in life. I know I'm in the wrong place. I feel it. It's an endless drain on me."

"It doesn't show," Bill started.

"Thank you but, as soon as I'm able, I mean to go somewhere else, and do something different."

Bill was a little wounded by this, "You don't mean that."

"Why not? Of course I do."

"Where will you go?"

"I don't know. New York, maybe. Could be Los Angeles."

"But you're so good here!"

"I'm not happy though Bill. That's what I wanted to tell you, since you are lost with me. If you are good at something but it doesn't make you happy, find a way to do something else. Do the thing that will make you happy," she finished with excitement.

Bill was swept up in her excitement. He knew the thing that would make him happy. He had a crush on this woman since middle school, and now she'd come all the way to his house to tell him to do the thing that would make him happy. It was an easy calculation to make. He grabbed Bella and tried to kiss her.

She elbowed Bill in the ribs and shoved him away, "No, Bill. No."

"I...I am so sorry!" he felt guilty and embarrassed, "I thought you were hinting... I was wrong. Just wrong."

"You were wrong," she echoed, "but I can accept your apology. You sound like you meant it."

"Bella, I just thought being with you is the thing that would make me happy."

"Me? That's ridiculous."

"I know, I know. I'm a nobody..."

"No. I am."

"You're Bella Clapford," he said, "You run the show. Of course you're somebody. Who am I?"

"You're my friend," she cleared her throat, "Nothing more than that, mind you."

"Yes. Again I'm sorry."

"Never mind that. Let's re-focus on the problem at hand. What makes you happy, Bill?"

"Well, now I'm not so sure."

"Oh...I see," she pondered a second realizing she should have left already, "I need to go," she said abruptly.

Bill didn't know how to respond. He felt exposed and embarrassed like he'd accidentally run into the middle of a busy intersection. She left before he said anything at all.

The next day at the plant Bill was worried about running into Bella all day. He was tense all day, assuming the inevitable would come sooner or later and there would need to be some sort of action taken. Disciplinary action, termination, demotion—something bad was bound to be coming for him.

One does not profess a love for the boss *to* the boss, especially when the boss is the sublime and untouchable Bella Clapford, without causing a ripple or two.

Wayne Curtis walked up to him with an order to be approved.

"This looks awful," Bill said.

"Excuse me?" Wayne bristled.

"Your colors are wrong, things are crooked. I can't think of a way this could be worse."

"That's a hell of a thing to say," Wayne started to get angry, "You know, you have the easiest job in this place. Anybody can stand around and nitpick, find things wrong with other people's work, especially if they're not doing any work themselves."

"Not doing any work?" Bill stood up and faced Wayne.

"I said what I said."

Bill handed Wayne his papers back, "Fix it."

Wayne stormed off and took out his anger whacking a side panel of the press with a crescent wrench a few times.

Bill collapsed back into his chair. He felt silly. He mentally ran through all the things wrong with that brochure again, and found even more he hadn't mentioned.

The rest of the day passed without incident. There were also no Bella Clapford sightings. Bill felt so much tension over what had happened the night before, he thought he'd have chosen to get fired just to know the outcome and avoid all the godawful tension.

Then he heard a knock at the door, and he regretted entertaining the thought that he'd rather get fired.

He opened the door to find Bella there. He lowered his eyes and braced for the rottenness to come.

"Hi Bill," she said cheerfully, "Mind if I come in?" The tone did not meet the situation, Bill thought, *She is about to gleefully fire me.*

"Come on in," he gestured meekly. He stood in the middle of the room and assumed a posture he imagined would somehow decrease the impact of the words.

"I've decided something, Bill," she said, "Since we spoke yesterday I've been thinking we can help one another. We can be partners in finding ourselves."

"Finding ourselves?" Bill was confused. This statement also did not square with the situation.

"We can help each other. We can talk once a week or so about where we're headed and why. Maybe talking it out is enough to help, maybe we give one another advice."

Bill was relieved, "You want my advice?"

"Well sure, don't you want mine?"

"Yes, yes of course," Bill said.

"Well then, let's get started," she said.

For weeks, Bella came to Bill's home once a week. She would talk him through career navigation and he would listen to her perform a monologue and tell her what he thought of it.

Neither of them was an expert, in spite of Bella's success. She'd been born into a life that secured her future. She was talented, which was a blessing for her company, but she would have been running it come what may.

Just so for Bill. He'd been born into a life where success was unlikely. The kinds of advice Bella was prepared to offer had little bearing on his situation.

He in turn knew nothing of acting. He'd seen it happening, he supposed. It was all over the television. What Bella was doing didn't seem to line up with that. He didn't know if that was a good or bad thing. He couldn't imagine a sitcom delivery of "tomorrow and tomorrow and tomorrow," though he tried.

In spite of their mutual blindness each felt the other was improving.

"We are ready," Bella said one night.

"We're ready?" Bill echoed.

"Yes. We're ready to go unleash what we've learned on the world. You're ready to go out and move up in the world. I'm ready to go become an actor. We owe it to ourselves and to one another to go take a serious stab at it."

"But what does that mean?"

"You've got to try for that management position we're opening."

"Okay, I can do that. What do you have to do?"

"I'm going to California."

"You're...what?"

"If I can make it there, Bill, I can make it anywhere."

"I suppose..."

"No more self doubt," she said inventing a mantra in such a way it sounded like something they'd been repeating to one another every week.

"Let's go set the world on fire then," Bill said smiling nervously.

Bella didn't see his nerves. She interpreted enthusiasm and she found it inspiring. She went straight home and packed her bags.

The next morning she drove to the airport in Louisville, found a flight for Los Angeles and bought a ticket.

On her flight she dreamed of casual conversations with the world's most famous set.

Bill went in to work the next day full of grim determination. He was going to let anyone who would listen know he was interested in and applying for the open management position. The job was ordering supplies and maintaining inventory on paper, ink, etc. He thought he could manage that easily enough.

He walked into the offices and asked to speak with Bella Clapford. The receptionist told him Bella was on a leave of absence out west.

"Who do I speak to about the management position?" Bill asked.

"That'd be Bella," the receptionist said.

"And she's not here. So who do I speak to in her absence?"

"I'm not sure, Bill," he said, "I'll find out and chase you down later today."

It wasn't the payoff Bill was looking for. After a long morning of putting himself in the right headspace to stick his neck out for the very first time, he'd expected something to happen.

Later that day Mike Taylor came to see him. Mike was a sales manager who oversaw all of the account executives in the place. He was the sort of man who had strong opinions about how to button the jacket of a suit. To him Bill Stegner was always going to be what he'd always been: no one of consequence.

"Harry at the front desk said you were asking about the management position," Mike said.

"I was," Bill said proudly.

"Why were you asking about it?" Mike asked. He asked it simply. Bill read into it that he couldn't conceive of a world where Bill was a viable candidate for that job.

He could feel himself shrinking.

"I wanted to know how to apply for it," Bill said quietly.

"Oh, well," Mike smiled, "You know someone who'd be interested in applying?"

"I do," Bill said, "Me."

Mike blurted out a laugh and tried to catch it before Bill heard it. The damage was already done.

Bill continued, "I've been speaking with Bella about this, and she told me to apply."

"Bella isn't here," Mike said.

"I'm aware," Bill said.

"Since she's not here, I think I'm the one making the decision about who gets that job."

"I see. And you've already written me off."

"Well, Bill..." he thought about his words carefully, "Why do you think you're the right person for this?"

"Bella said so."

"Great! Bella thinks you're right for the job. Do you think so?"

"Well..." it was a point Bill hadn't considered.

"You see?" Mike smiled, "Self doubt. You're going to have to do something about that before you start moving on."

Bill sort of agreed with that, which surprised himself. None of this was what he wanted or imagined, and yet it all felt like it was making sense to him. He felt like a turkey agreeing to be Thanksgiving dinner.

He still half-heartedly put his name in for the promotion. He did not hear more about the job until it was announced that Wayne Curtis was going to be the new inventory manager.

Bill sighed, congratulated Wayne, and settled back into his life the way it was before Bella had started working with him.

After a month or so Bella showed back up at the plant and resumed her life running the company. Bill came to visit her in her office. Harry sighed at him and let him go in.

"How was California?" Bill asked hopefully.

"I'd rather not discuss it," she said, "What about the management position?"

"Let's not talk about it," Bill said.

They both sat in an embarrassing silence for a few beats.

"Well... I'm glad you're back," Bill said.

"Sure," she nodded mechanically, "It's good to be back."

Ghost in the Graveyard

In the third grade, my whole class became fascinated with ghosts and cemeteries. We learned all the unwritten rules you could think of about cemeteries and ghosts. Some we made up ourselves. It was a collaborative effort developing and cataloguing all of these rules. The entire class was involved in one way or another. It was not an obsession, we would be playing or doing something else, and someone might say, "So speaking of ghosts," which we hadn't been, "my brother told me something last night," and just like that everyone was interested. It was an easy way to get people's attention, and everyone played.

Some notable rules were:

Don't stand on a person's grave, or that person's ghost will haunt you.

If you spit near someone's grave, that person will haunt you.

If you shake someone's hand in a cemetery, the Devil will raise all the dead in that cemetery to haunt you if you should break your word.

If you fall asleep in a cemetery, you will vanish into a fiery pit and never be heard from again.

I used to wonder about the boundaries of a cemetery. The one next to my friend Jason's house was hardly an exact geometric shape. The back and side boundaries were the forest. The trees had been cleared out in a nearly exact rectangle to allow space for the parsonage and burial plots. On the front side there were peninsulas of gravesites jutting out all over the place.

One peninsula stuck out from behind the house, and down the side, extending all the way to the road.

Is the boundary like a coastline, and it goes wherever the headstones are, like the coast of Norway? Or did it need a more standard geometric shape to achieve the proper reverence? I imagined a diagonal line cutting from where the cemetery met the road, through to the back corner of the cemetery behind the house.

It cut the house in half.

Jason's family lived in the parsonage directly across from the Church where his father was minister. His family had every episode of the original series of *Star Trek* on VHS in their house. They hadn't recorded them from television, they were purchased: officially curated!

They were the definition of cool as far as I was concerned.

In third grade, Jason and I had been content to play near the cemetery, regurgitating our complex, ghost-based mythology.

Voodoo in the minister's house.

This last rule about falling asleep in a cemetery was the reason I was so concerned with cemetery boundaries. What a cruel fate for my friend or his family to be caught unaware sleeping in a cemetery due to some administrative oversight about where the boundary actually fell. I was glad Jason's bedroom was on the side of the house that wasn't involved in the cemetery no matter where you cared to draw its boundaries. Otherwise he might fall asleep inside the boundary and disappear forever.

We really believed that then.

I don't mean to give the impression I couldn't tell the difference between make-believe and reality. My inadequate little brain just reasoned that make-believe was a private thing. We did all sorts of make-believe games at home, my siblings and I. No one else was involved, and we all understood what we were up to. The common world, the "out there" we share with other people was not a venue for make-believe. There was no deception out there. If someone was willing to share something with you, and they weren't your sibling, whatever it might be, it wasn't make-believe. That meant all this talk of graveyards and ghosts and hauntings must be real.

As time passed, mentions of these cemetery rules faded away. It was like we came back from summer break into fourth grade and couldn't remember what topics of conversation used to fill our time. Or maybe those topics of conversation were just replaced by whatever new martial arts centered soap-opera-for-kids had debuted that summer. For everyone else, this meant no new fuel added to the fire of the ghost laws, and they just died. For me this meant there was no new evidence to challenge the rules we had or establish any new ones, so they just sort of lingered out there like mathematical axioms that never cease being true whether they get to be applied or not.

By fifth grade, my classmates had completely moved on. Those third-grade superstitions were considered too childish to discuss. We no longer mentioned what would happen to your children and grandchildren if you happened to urinate on a headstone. Fair enough, I thought. How often do you need to remind yourself the Pythagorean Theorem is true?

So the ghost laws remained unchallenged, and I held onto them in spite of my nickname, which was Spock. They would have called me illogical if I had mentioned it.

It was around this time that the truth about Santa began to be publicly discussed. Some of us found out earlier than others and politely kept it to ourselves until this point. I guess we all felt the cat was out of the bag, no use pretending.

I had been a Santa believer like most of my classmates, too. I had to come to terms with the ugly truth we all must come to terms with on an ongoing basis. Some of the things we thought were true end up not being so, and the ones we know about are just the ones we've uncovered so far. We all believe a great many false things, most likely. I did start to question whether "Don't use the middle finger in a cemetery or Satan will kick you in the balls" was of the same epistemic ilk as "one plus one is two." I was too embarrassed to ask in case I was way off base.

I was embarrassed about most things anyway. My family couldn't afford for all of us to go to see movies in theaters, so a great many animated films my classmates had seen in theaters were already out on VHS, bought, watched, worn out, yawned at and being used for doorstops before I saw them for the first time. I couldn't relate to them on most cultural topics. The one exception was broadcast television which, like death, comes to us all.

Even at school I didn't have common ground. I was in the elementary school's Gifted & Talented program, which was an accelerated learning program. So my homework had nothing to do with that of my classmates.

I shared a bedroom with all three of my siblings. I don't know if I was the only one with this kind of arrangement. I was afraid to ask. In practically every way, my life had become out of sync with my friends, and I wasn't sure if we were friends anymore.

I was an outcast.

Still, I managed an invitation to the coolest party in all the fifth grade: my best friend Jason's birthday party.

The invitation was canary yellow with black ink. The font was wide, and all of the letters were capitalized. Capitalization meant excitement. Capitalization meant games. Capitalization meant cake.

It read

BIRTHDAY PARTY!!! PLEASE COME AND JOIN US THIS FRIDAY FOR CAKE PARTY GAMES AND BONFIRE

My imagination outdid itself in anticipation. When I received my invitation, Jason said, "My mom said a few people could sleep over. You can sleep over if you want."

I spent much of the rest of that week anticipating all kinds of possibilities for how this would go down.

Scenario 1: Since I was Jason's best friend, and everybody knew it, they would be giving *me* gifts as well as Jason. Perhaps even *The Lion King* on VHS!

Scenario 2: Being Jason's best friend, I was bound to have some sort of seat of honor at the party. Everyone in the whole class would suddenly look up to me. My previously bizarre ways would become the fad. Everyone would emulate me.

And then I would have the chance to say, "Yes, but there's only one original...."

Scenario 3: We would watch old *Star Trek* episodes. Our classmates would fall in love with it. I could finally find out what in the world a "tribble" was, and everyone who didn't realize it before would see how truly Spock-like I was. Of course, they would secretly admire me for it.

It rained for three days before the party. All of the firewood that had been intended for the bonfire was soaked and couldn't be used, Jason's dad said.

In spite of the soggy earth, the party was still held outdoors. Nearly the entire class had been invited, and only one person who had been invited failed to show: Dawson, the class bully, who had chicken pox.

Serves him right.

Jason's parents couldn't fit all of us inside their house. They tried their best to keep us entertained and under control. We played games—church youth group games like Romans & Christians: an execution-less sanitized version of real historical horrors.

We quickly grew bored and restless.

Parents of the more outer-circle set of Jason's friends started showing up to pick up their children. There was a scarcely mistakable hierarchy of friendship levels in that. The longer you stayed, the more you were in. These were the people who were leaving after only an hour. I was staying overnight.

Jason's parents decided that this would be a good time to open presents. This way the people who were leaving could see their gift being opened, and the party would be dwindling down to a size that didn't call for meticulous supervision.

That seemed a practical time to hand out presents, but was, in fact, a hideously effective way of torturing children.

Naturally, the gifts from people who were leaving were handed out first. Some of them hadn't brought any gifts, and so were forced to leave with a reasonable amount of embarrassment.

Jason was given video games, movies, action figures, and remote control cars.

The gift giving moved up through the social hierarchy of the party. Getting to the overnight guests at the end. My gift was the very last one, I don't mind saying.

My parents had picked out, purchased, and wrapped the gift that I brought. I didn't even know what it was. It was this: a jigsaw puzzle that, when pieced together after hours of aggravating tedium, would form a parrot.

Even the parrot on the box seemed bored by the prospect.

It wasn't the grand finale to gift opening everyone had hoped for. I apologized to my friend.

"Oh no, it's okay I guess," he said. His parents gave him a look, "Thank you," he added.

Jason's parents went back inside, and he turned to us. With an air of mischief he said, "Let's play a game."

A game of our own choosing, with no parental consent. It could be anything forbidden—Poker, Blackjack, Roulette, real tackle football...

"Ghost in the Graveyard," Jason said.

My heart skipped a few beats. My blood ran cold. I swore silently with a few words that had never been used before.

Going into the graveyard to play was very much against our third grade rules, and as far as I knew they were still hanging out there in Platonic heaven, warning little kids not to do damn foolish things like play in a graveyard.

I had never heard of the game, but neither had anyone else. I felt slightly validated by that. For once, I was not alone in my social ignorance.

Jason said he was making the game up, "Well, there might be a game called 'Ghost in the Graveyard', but it's not this one." He began to lay out the rules. One person was picked to be the ghost. That person went into the cemetery to hide, while everyone else counted to 50. When the rest of us got to 50, we would set out to find the ghost, if they were found and tagged before they could tag anyone else, they had to be the ghost again. Otherwise, whoever they tagged had to be the new ghost.

Jason volunteered to be the ghost first. I was not chosen and this all seemed like a bad and horrifying idea so I excused myself to go hide in the bathroom.

I paced back and forth in fear in Jason's bathroom for a long while. Eventually, someone tried to open the door. It was Jason's mother.

I flushed the toilet and washed my hands to disguise the fact that I hadn't been up to any business in there.

Jason's mother kept waiting for me at the door.

"You've been in there an awful long time," she said.

"Yeah, I really had to go."

"Really?"

"Yeah...I had to poop."

"Well, when you're done in there, everyone's still outside," she sighed.

Feeling that I had committed some egregious social error, I stammered that I would be going outside. As I opened the door I began to cry. I was crying the tears of a child who's been forced to do something they genuinely don't want to do: put down their dog, give away their toys, play a game with their friends in a cemetery. I was sobbing by the time I got to edge of the cemetery.

My classmates were all engaged in the game, looking for the ghost, and paid no attention to me, very obviously not suffering any cosmic consequences due to their actions. "When is hellfire going to rain down on them from above?" I wondered.

I ran sobbing straight through the cemetery to the furthest corner, where no one was looking, and stopped. I caught my breath and looked down. What I saw made me stop crying.

No one had found the first ghost. Jason had waited for a long time to be found, and he had fallen asleep with his arms and legs around a headstone. He had not fallen into a fiery pit.

This was the exact moment I began to think like an adult, "I'm so stupid," I said out loud.

This was enough to wake Jason, "Huh? What?" he said. Then I guess he remembered why he was in the cemetery and what we were doing.

He slapped the back of my leg and yelled "YOU'RE IT!"

The Chicken Detective

I met Mr. Preston one morning in December when we had some bad weather. The little lane running back into my neighborhood had iced over completely. I decided to try to make it out of the neighborhood anyway hoping the main roads would be clear. I started out relatively okay, and made it almost to the road before my car slid sideways across the road through the grass in Mr. Preston's yard, and ended up sitting perched on a rock overlooking a deep drainage ditch.

I tried reversing and flooring it, only digging deeper holes in Mr. Preston's yard. He heard all the motor revving from inside his kitchen and came out to see what had happened to his property. I got out of my car and stood by the road, waiting for him to walk down to where I was stuck.

Mr. Preston was around 70 years old, retired, with the face of a pleasant banker. He had donned a navy blue canvas jacket and brown trapper hat before coming down to see me. He had dressed in blue jeans and a thick flannel shirt that morning for other reasons. I did not find out what they were.

"Looks like you're stuck," he said in that midwestern tone that sounds so polite it masks that the words themselves are kind of neutral and agnostic about politeness. It's a gift that we all share, and it's convinced the world that we're far more polite than we actually are.

"Yeah, I lost traction on the ice," I said in the same tone.

"You call a tow truck yet?" he asked turning and looking intently at me.

"No, I don't have a cell phone," I said.

"Looks like you dug some ruts in my yard," he said turning around looking at the four muddy lines leading from the ice to my car.

"Oh, I'm sorry," I said, "like I said I lost traction."

"Uh-huh. I heard you gunning your engine out here too."

"Yeah, again, I'm sorry about that. I thought I'd be able to get out on my own."

He looked at me as I were stupid. "Your car is perched up on a rock," he said pointing at the rock.

I felt smaller than a flea's sneeze. "Well, I'm sorry. I didn't know about the rock. I just thought..."

"Don't worry," he said chuckling, "You're okay. Your car didn't slide down in that ditch. You're lucky. You can come back this spring when it warms up and help me patch up the yard, and I'll call it even. Right now, I'll call a tow truck. Why don't you come on up to the porch and we'll wait for the truck up there."

It was at this point that I first saw the rooster. On his front porch, Mr. Preston had a three-foot-tall cement rooster painted in ostentatious blues, reds, greens, yellows, and oranges. It stood upright surveying the world as if it were all its kingdom, his chest puffed out and his rudely bright tail feathers broadcasted boldly from behind. It was the exact attitude living and breathing roosters adopt when they are trying to demonstrate their acceptability as a mate to some impressionable young hen.

I could not believe I never noticed it as I drove by twice a day. It was gaudy and hideous. It was unlike anything else in our drab, sedate little town full of browns and grays. It was especially unlike what I had learned about Mr. Preston in our brief conversation next to my car.

"I've never noticed this rooster before," I said.

"Oh that's Leroy."

"Leroy?"

"Yep. I named him."

That was a little odd, but fine by me. It's none of my business if this man wants to name his cement rooster, "I see."

"You probably think that's a little bit kooky."

"Not especially."

"I got this rooster for kids to do a prank."

"You did?"

"Yeah. You see, the high school kids, they can come and take the rooster off my porch and hide it somewhere. Then I've got to go and find it, bring it back, and the next school year, a new class gets to come and steal my rooster and hide it somewhere."

"Ahh I see. Kind of an annual tradition."

"That's it!"

"That's kind of neat," I said, "How many times has it been taken?"

"Oh, they haven't taken it yet."

"I see. Well it's, mid-year for them, still plenty of time to get it in by the end of the year. How long have you had Leroy?" I felt odd being on first-name basis with an inanimate object.

"Ohh," he said pausing to think, "I guess about ten years."

"Ten years! They haven't taken it in all this time?"

"No, I figure it will just start happening one year and this prank can get going then."

"Does anyone know they're supposed to steal it?"

"Well, no," he said thoughtfully, "I just assumed people would *want* to take the ugliest cement rooster in town, he turned to the rooster, "No offense Leroy."

I didn't find it as odd about being on first name basis with Leroy then. At least I wasn't the one worried about hurting his feelings.

He went inside and called the tow truck. We sat on the porch and waited. He brought me out a cup of coffee when he emerged. While we waited he asked me all the standard general information questions: did I have any kids, was I married, was I seeing someone, just not working out for me eh, where did I work, how long had I been there, where did I go to school, what did I study, etc.

After about fifteen minutes the tow truck emerged at the mouth of our road. It turned to come down to Mr. Preston's, and as it made the turn on the ice, the momentum of the truck carried it sideways across the ice into the ditch on the far side. A second truck had to be called to pull out the first truck. By the time the drivers finally got it all worked out, the sun angles had shifted, and the ice was starting to thin out. A third truck was finally able to get in to pull my car out.

For reasons I will never understand, they weren't able to pull my car back out the direction it went in, so the driver pulled it out diagonally going in the forward direction. Making my four existing mud lines in the Preston yard into 4 muddy V's, and doubling the damage I'd done.

"It's all right," said Mr. Preston, "You can help me fix that too when you come back in the spring," he reassured me.

That March I stopped by one Saturday morning to ask Mr. Preston when he thought a good time to fix his yard would be. Before I got out of my car, I saw him on his front porch pacing up and down. He looked excited in an unexpected way, like if a tortoise were doing a jig. It seemed he bounced back and forth between an excitement of anticipation and excitement from worry. He was all energy, pacing back and forth, rubbing his hands together, discussing something animatedly with, well the molecules that surround us all, I imagine. There was no other person around. He had a smile on his face at one point, and a look of deep concern on his face at another. It was peculiar.

I got out of my car.

"Hallo, Mr. Preston!"

He stopped pacing and stared at me for a few seconds before any glimmer of recognition flickered across his face, "Ah yes, the yard destroyer!" This was said gruffly, and very much *not* in that comforting midwestern tone of politeness.

"Yes, well about that...."

"Look!" he shouted, "Someone's taken Leroy!"

"Hey, that's great!"

"Is it?" he asked.

"I thought that's why you wanted it: for the pranks."

"Yes, but how in the devil am I going to find it again?"

"Do you own a spaceship? Cause I think you could see it from the moon."

"Jokes are no help right now."

"Sorry."

"Well? Do you have any ideas on how to find this thing?"

"You wanted this prank to go on, but you never thought about how to hunt for the rooster after it was taken?"

"This is no time for sass."

"Sorry."

"No, I'm sorry. I didn't think anyone would *actually* ever take Leroy and now he's gone, and...I don't know, I guess I'm kind of embarrassed."

"What?"

"That I never thought it through. I'm kind of caught with my pants down, aren't I?"

"Look, I'll help. I'll drive around and look in yards and let you know what I can see."

"Would you? That would be a tremendous help!" he exclaimed.

"Sure," I said.

"And listen," he said, getting an idea, "they'll return to the scene of the crime. So come back tonight at eleven and wear some camouflage."

"I don't own any camo!" I said. In hindsight I can say I was worried about the wrong part of that request.

"Run out and get some" he said, "and be back here at eleven. You can hunt for Leroy while you're out."

"Okay..." I said, wondering how I'd gotten roped into all of this.

"Great. See you tonight."

I guess the yard wasn't a priority anymore. He went back in his house, and I walked back to my car, befogged by the momentum of the thing.

I drove around that afternoon, running my new errand of picking out some camouflage clothing to wear that night, in the dark, when no one would be able to see us anyway. On my way home I drove down every road or alley or side street in Hardy I could think of, but did not see Leroy anywhere. I even drove out west of town where there's a sort of tourist farm called Felson's. People can go there to pick their own berries, or see how wine is made, and generally feel "country" without having to get very involved in the reality of the lifestyle. There are billboards for it all over Clapford County.

There was no sign of Leroy there, either.

I showed up at Mr. Preston's just before eleven. On my arrival, he looked out into his driveway and decided the extra car looked suspicious. So he told me to take my car back to my house and walk back. It was only about a quarter of a mile, so I didn't mind.

I drove down and walked the quarter mile back to Mr. Preston's house. It was one of those walks where circumstances make you really take a hard look at your life. It wasn't the most fruitful think, but I thought anyway. I hadn't had very good answers about who I was dating or where I was working, or what I was doing with my life when he asked me, back when we first met. I thought about how it was because I was the sort of fool who would agree to meet some old man in the night wearing camouflage because a statue-stealer might re-appear. *Maybe I should make some changes*, I thought to myself.

When I got back to Mr. Preston's he was waiting for me at the end of his driveway.

"Come with me," he said.

He led me across the street into the wooded area straight out from his front porch. In the woods there he'd set up a duck blind—sort of a camouflage tent—for us to hide inside and still keep an eye on the door. I wondered why I needed to buy camo then, if we were going to be hidden inside a camo tent in the dark.

"This is exciting," he said.

"Yep," I said very half-heartedly.

"When I was in school, there were always pranks like this going on," he said, "My father would have beat me within an inch of my life if he found out I was involved in one. Military man," he said as if that were an explanation.

"I never did any either," I said. Mr. Preston did not seem interested.

"I used to own the general store in town. The food mart you know it?"

"Yeah I know it."

"I always hired high school kids down there and, you know, they always talked about pranks that had happened in school."

"Uh-huh, like I said..."

"It sure was exciting hearing them talk about them."

"I can see that."

"Anyway, I can't believe I finally get to be part of one!"

"So," I ventured, "what happens if they don't come back tonight."

"Eh? Well, ummm, they always return to the sign of the crime don't they?"

"I don't know."

"I mean, maybe not tonight. But we'll set up tomorrow night too, if we have to."

"Oh..." the thought of doing this indefinitely every night for the rest of our days flashed through my brain.

"Look, I know you think I'm a crazy old man. I really appreciate you sitting out here with me. Since Cheryl died, I don't get a lot of visitors you know."

"Was Cheryl—"

"My wife," he said, "She passed away two years ago."

"Oh I'm sorry," I said, and I meant it.

"Well, anyway," he said. That seemed to be the end of the matter as far as he was concerned. He moved on with the conversation, "Why do you just let things happen to you?"

"I don't...uh, do that."

"Why are you sitting here right now?"

"I'm helping you catch the rooster thief."

"What's it to you though? I mean I just snapped my fingers, and you're going to sit up all night with me? Who am I to you?"

"I'm invested now. I have to know how this all plays out," I said.

"Tell yourself that I guess," he said, "but sooner or later you're going to have to grow a pair and choose your own path."

"I do that."

"Uh-huh," I hadn't convinced either of us.

We sort of sat in silence after that. I had no good retort, and frankly I was pretty sore at him for having me pegged so exactly and hitting on the exact sore thread that had been weighing on me all damn day. How do I end up in these situations? I just don't get myself out of them. It seems like it would be easy enough to make my excuses, right now, and stand up and go home. But for some reason I chose to let someone else dictate the terms, and that led me to staying up all night in a duck blind with a stranger who lives in my neighborhood, waiting for someone who almost certainly wasn't coming back to the porch.

By five AM, nothing had happened. We were both just exhausted.

"Tonight we'll take shifts watching," Mr. Preston said as we left the duck blind.

"Okay sounds good," I said, too tired to start standing up for myself now.

The quarter mile walk I hadn't minded the previous night seemed like an eternity in the morning. I decided not to do any soul searching on this trip, just get home and crawl into bed.

I slept until about three in the afternoon, ate a little food, and kept thinking about Leroy. The idea that this rooster was stolen as part of a high school prank just didn't sit right with me, even though that was the whole reason it sat on Mr. Preston's porch. You can't just think a thing into existence. Not really. I mean, someone may have a vision board at home that inspires them to work harder, something like that. Even then, the vision didn't make the person get the stuff, the hard work did.

Nevertheless, someone did steal that rooster. Why? I couldn't make sense of it, and I didn't like how much of my headspace it was taking up. I decided to take a drive and clear my head. Maybe, while I was out, I could peak around and see if I could find that rooster. At least if the thing was solved I wouldn't have to think about it anymore.

I drove around, but I didn't find anything but the same old dreary drabness Hardy is constantly draped in. A beautiful season of rebirth and renewal like Spring is felt all around, and simultaneously manages not to brighten up a single thing.

I went home empty handed and waited until nightfall to walk over to Mr. Preston's to resume our watch. He met me again at the end of his driveway, "It occurred to me we can see the front porch just fine from the living room. We don't have to hide across the street and stay outside all night. I just need to open the blinds a little bit."

"That sounds marvelous."

We went inside, and I got a view of Mr. Preston's home for the very first time. Neat as a pin is how I'd describe it, so far as I could see anyway. He walked us in to a sitting room that was simply decorated with a wedding photo of what I assumed was the Prestons, a grandfather clock standing tall and stately, and a bookshelf half filled with historical fiction, half with books about the civil war. That must just happen to men around here at a certain age. They run out and read all they can about Abraham Lincoln and Robert E. Lee.

There was a picture window overlooking the porch. In front of this were positioned two very cozy-looking recliners.

"Say, this is better than the duck blind," I said.

"Yes. We need to find Leroy. I don't know why we have to get back pains along the way."

I pitched his idea of taking shifts, and Mr. Preston thought that was marvelous. I offered to take the first shift and he agreed. He was sawing logs by five after. So I prepared for a long vigilant watch. I set to imitating the action of the tiger, as Shakespeare said. I stiffened the sinews and summoned up the blood.

I fell asleep by eleven fifteen.

The chairs may have swung the pendulum too far in the comfort direction.

I woke up shortly after six in the morning. A shower was running, and for some reason an old man was singing "Auld Lang Syne."

I blinked out the window, and there was a note taped to the glass. I tried blinking again, but it was still there.

I walked out onto the porch, got the note, and read it:

I HAVE YOUR CHICKEN

-PETE

Mystery solved, I thought. Pete has it. Now we only needed to figure out who Pete was, and we'd be set.

In a few short minutes, Mr. Preston emerged from the bathroom fully dressed in his familiar blue jeans and plaid flannel shirt, with his hair neatly plastered down and parted to the side.

"Good morning," he said, "I didn't wake you up did I?"

"I don't think so," I said, "But listen, Pete left you a note." I'd hoped the name would mean something to him.

"Who's Pete?" he asked.

"Oh I don't know, but he has your chicken," I gave him the sheet of paper from the window.

"Oh *that* Pete."

I was stunned, "You knew who had your chicken this whole time?"

"Eh, no. But if you say someone named Pete has it, well there's only one Pete it could be: Pete Felson."

"Felson? From the farm west of town?" I remembered seeing the billboards.

"Yes. Pete went to school with me."

"But how long ago was that? That can't be why he took Leroy," there I went with that first name basis again.

"Meet me at the high school at five," he said.

"You got it," I said.

I pulled in to the parking lot at Walter Clapford High School just before five, and Mr. Preston was there already, waiting outside his car with his arms crossed, still dressed in the same flannel and jeans as this morning. His attitude just a bit more...determined than before.

I parked and got out of the car.

"Lawn wrecker," he said.

"Mr. Preston," I said.

"This might get violent," he said. I found this funny. Two seventy-somethings coming to blows over a cement rooster did not seem probable or advisable. I let out a small chuckle. "I'm serious. There is more to this than a cement rooster."

"Like what?"

"It's...it's private, and maybe it won't come up, but we have a lot of history and this fella used to be a bully," he said.

"Right, but that was forty-five years ago," I said, politely forgetting ten whole years or more.

"I told you my father was a military man. He didn't stand for any fighting in school. He wanted discipline. So I never stood up to this sumbitch and he thinks I'm a pushover. Well, he's got another think coming."

I saw a different level of resolve in Mr. Preston's face than I had seen before. So I decided to just pipe down and ready myself for whatever might happen.

A farm truck crested the hill and came down into the parking lot and pulled into a spot nose-to-nose with Mr. Preston's car. Pete Felson got out of the car and took a glance at me.

"Did you bring someone to do your fighting for you?" He jeered. As farm life goes, it had been relatively kind to Pete Felson, he did not appear as weathered or leathery as most farmers in the area do. He looked, like Mr. Preston, like a business man who spent most of his time at a desk. The nature of operating a tourist farm, I suppose.

"There's not going to be any fighting," Mr. Preston said.

"What's *he* here for then, Bill?" Bill? His name was Bill? I was relieved to finally know the man's first name, but it also occurred to me he'd never asked mine.

"The rooster was his idea," Mr. Preston - Bill - was improvising, "and he wants to see it returned."

"Well hang on, we're not to the damn rooster yet," Pete said.

"All right," said Mr. Preston.

"You can't buy my farm," my neck turned so quick at this statement it hurt. Felson's was for sale? Mr. Preston wanted to buy it? What was all this? History indeed!

"Pete, you're going under. Don't destroy everything you built just because you don't want me to be the one to buy your farm."

"Someone else will want to buy."

"Don't be ridiculous, just take the money and retire."

"I am going to beat you silly," Pete said.

"No you're not, don't be an idiot."

"An Idiot? Huh, an idiot am I?" Pete Felson took a swing at Mr. Preston. Now, an old man punch is something that you have to see to believe, Pete came in with a haymaker, a big hook that was once very mighty. You could just tell from the confidence with which he swung. It was now very avoidable and slow.

Mr. Preston easily stepped to the outside of the punch, let Pete's momentum take him of balance, and then kicked him—honest to god, he kicked him—the rest of the way off balance onto the ground.

Pete Felson was all fury and bewilderment, "What the hell?" he said, repeating, "What the hell?" The scenario did not add up to him, and he really struggled to come to terms with what had just happened.

"See if Leroy's in the truck," Mr. Preston said.

"What the hell?" asked Pete, struggling to get to his feet.

I walked around to the back of the truck and there was Leroy wrapped in burlap. I picked him and carried him to the back of Mr. Preston's car.

"What the hell?" said Pete, failing to find something new to say, but now back to standing position.

"You thought," said Mr. Preston, "all these years I was a pushover because my dad wouldn't let me fight you. I'm not scared of you. I was never scared of you. Take the offer, if you're not a moron. If you are a moron, don't take it. But leave the damn chicken out of it," he said and turned to make a dramatic exit, although there were logistical matters to care for, such as loading the rooster in the car, that spoiled his speech somewhat.

"The rooster," Pete said. He turned toward me, marched over and kicked Leroy as hard as he could, knocking him over and breaking his neck. His head popped off and slid across the parking lot.

Rest in peace, Leroy.

I looked up at his crazed smile of satisfaction at having had some small piece of victory amidst all this defeat, and I swung.

I swung for justice and for Leroy, my departed friend.

I caught Pete Felson right in the jaw with a swift, if not powerful, jab that knocked him down.

"Kid!" said Mr. Preston.

"I don't know what happened! He just..."

"Get in the car," he said.

"Oh! Good idea," I said.

"What the hell?" Pete was asking again.

We both got in our cars and drove back to his house. We didn't plan to go there, it just seemed like the best place for me to go after all of that.

"You grew a pair," Mr. Preston said, excited.

"I don't know what came over me."

"I'm glad you did, kid. Don't let people push you around."

"Right," I said, "So what happens next?"

"I got a load of dirt coming next Saturday, you can come by and help me fill in these ruts in my yard."

"Yes sir," I said.

When I came by the following week to fix the yard, sitting on the porch was a brand new cement rooster, painted somehow more ostentatiously than Leroy was.

"You got a new Leroy?" I asked.

"Yep, it was a present from Pete when he accepted my offer to buy his farm. I'm going to bury the old one down there, at the farm."

GLUE

Against the heat of summer, the breeze felt perfect. Lola looked out from her father's deck and couldn't imagine a better moment. After running away for so long, her father could finally settle here and live easy. Even the weather seemed to be on their side.

Her dad and her husband John were in the garage drinking swill beer from the fridge out there. The Twins were playing on the TV. Part of learning to live easy was going to mean learning to love what the locals loved. Ice hockey, Vikings football, and Twins baseball.

The lake was a short walk from the deck, her dad's canoe was pulled on shore after a wobbly maiden voyage. None of the Petersons had very good balance in the boat, but they'd learn. They felt safe and had nothing but time now.

That afternoon they spent watching baseball, fishing, paddling, and just enjoying the calm and peace of the Minnesota air.

At the end of the day Lola and her husband said their goodbyes and drove out of the lane. She turned back to look at the cabin as they pulled away. As she did, she saw a man in a denim rancher jacket step out of the woods behind them. He had a rifle casually resting on his shoulder. He turned toward the cabin.

"John. Stop. A reaper."

"WHAT? Here?"

"You have to go back!" She screamed.

Another man stepped out of the woods and turned toward the cabin, then another, and another. John saw each of them.

"We're outnumbered. It's no use getting all of us killed."

"You can't just let my father die!"

"We can't stop it now."

"You don't know that! After everything we've been through to get here, to be safe, you can't just give up on him now."

Just then another man stepped out of the woods and turned towards the truck. John mashed on the gas pedal and sped away.

"No!" Lola screamed, but she felt the helplessness of the situation and cried. She pulled out her phone with shaky hands and dropped it onto the floor of John's truck.

"What are you doing?" he shouted.

"I'm trying to call the police!"

"What are they going to do?"

"Catch the bad guys," she said.

"They can't catch them. We tried that before, remember?"

"I don't know what else to do. Someone needs to know what's going on out here."

"All right, fine. Call them."

They heard several shots fire in rapid succession and then quiet—that eerie quiet of the woods when even the birds are startled and refuse to sing.

Lola called the police.

John drove straight toward town to until he saw a police cruiser coming from town with its lights on and then turned around and went back. He didn't want to show up at his father-in-law's house before the police got there.

They pulled up outside the house right behind the police officer. In the yard lay five dead reapers. Lola's father was nowhere to be found.

The reapers' guns were gone. There were no firearms found anywhere in the house. The police had questions, "Why did you follow us to the scene?"

"I'm the one who called this in," Lola said.

"Any relation to these folks?"

"No sir. This is my father's house, though. We saw these guys carrying shotguns in as we were on our way out. That's why we called. That and we heard the gunshots."

"You didn't come back?"

John answered, "We didn't know if it would be safe."

"That's not a bad decision. It's best to let us handle it. By the same token, you probably shouldn't have followed us in. Things could have gone sideways real quick."

"Yes sir. I understand sir."

"Stay here in the driveway, and don't touch anything. The situation seems okay right now. Call your father and see if you can get him back here. We have some questions we want to ask him. It's not great that he fled the scene, but it looks like, if what you say is true and these guys came in with shotguns, they were trying to get the best of him. I wouldn't feel safe sticking around here either. You go home, call him, and give us a call when you know something."

"I'll try," Lola said.

"Ask for Officer Schiltz. That's me."

"Yes sir."

Lola and John got back in their truck and started driving.

"What are you going to do? Your dad doesn't have a phone."

"I know. There's a lot about why that is that we can't explain to cops. Remember?"

"Well, no shit. What I mean is, they're going to call you asking for more information...what is your plan?"

"We'll have to find him."

"But now they'll be looking for us too."

"This wasn't supposed to happen," she said, sobbing.

"No...." John wanted to press on, but the promise of a new life here, clear of everything from before, to live in peace, it was all gone now. The reapers caught up to them anyway. The idea they might ever be free seemed delusional now.

Mathias Befton already knew the op had gone bad when there was no check-in within five minutes. He heard police cars, so he checked out of the motel, got in his Camry, and headed back to Indiana. It's best if I don't have to answer any questions, he thought. There was a copy of Osbert Solomon's *The Principles of Transcending Bliss* in his passenger seat. He reached his hand down and ran his thumb down the corner the pages absentmindedly as he drove.

This is pulling me back through bliss into the world, he thought. The world is always pulling you back. The world cannot handle the sublimely rational thought that beyond bliss, beyond happiness, peace, security, wellbeing, prosperity, all that fool's gold, beyond all of that is the truer, the realer, the beyond feelings so few humans see.

The world isn't comfortable with anyone moving beyond peace. They must prevent us from becoming, and from going beyond their comprehension. Purge the world. Confess. Confess. Confess.

He drove on through Minnesota, Wisconsin, Illinois, down into Indiana. Back to the GLUE compound in the center of Clapford County.

Befton arrived at the compound, parked his car, picked up his copy of Osbert Solomon, and walked into the Council Hall: a sort of pole barn structure they'd repurposed for official secretive business. It was cold in there in the winter. It was hot in the summers. The floors were concrete. Every sound echoed.

Rhee Stancroft saw him walk in. She dropped her pen, took her glasses off in a slow dramatic motion and took a long deep breath. Rhee and Mathias had a history, and a present. They had been having sex for ten years or so, stretching back to when he'd first taken on responsibility for training the Reapers. Back then she was trying to make it onto the Council, and she'd thought it would be politically expedient to start wooing the guy responsible for the entire organization's tactical might.

As time wore on, she realized he had no political savvy, or even awareness. He was useless as an ally, and forever doomed to be a muscle controlled by those more astute and more adept. But she was chained to him, so she thought she could at least try to be the one to control him.

The relationship had, on more than one occasion, proved uncomfortable, and this nonsense in Minnesota was disturbing to Rhee. In public areas of the compound, however, they had to appear neutral toward one another, a fact Rhee was grateful for.

He looked at her cavalierly, the effect of spending hours driving in meditation. He'd already moved beyond, onto the next problem. Rhee interpreted his attitude as cluelessness, and apathy about how bad this was.

"Was it The Rhino?" she asked.

He seemed frustrated by the question, "What do you think?"

"How would I know? I wasn't there. You were there. Was it him?"

"I wasn't there, really. I was in the hotel."

"WHAT?" she roared.

"These ops are dangerous, and these reapers are gifted. They don't need me. I trust my team to get the job done."

"Well they didn't."

"No. It went bad."

"So maybe in the future you maintain visual contact?"

"He took out five of them. He got away. The girl and her husband weren't even there. We have them to worry about too. I know everything I need to know. What do we gain by having me be in visual range?"

"Fine then. You don't know everything you need to know. You don't know where he went, but whatever you say, Befton. What's next?"

"I'm calling in the Llama."

She considered that for a moment, "Agreed. It's come to that. Send her in."

* _-*-_ *

Esther Cornwall was an expert on GLUE. She had been studying them from her time as a field agent twenty-five years ago. Her role became very consultative and data-oriented as her rank increased and reports of GLUE activity quieted down.

And now, after all this time her phone was ringing. There was a field agent—Sarah something-or-other—who was calling her office in Chicago and asking her for information about GLUE. After all this time, they needed a field agent, and Esther felt snubbed that she wasn't picked to go.

"There was this reaper in the eighties, he was called the Rhino, a real illusion master," she told Sarah.

"Illusion master?"

"He could make whatever he did look like whatever he wanted."

"Not following..."

"Well shut it. I'm telling you.

"In eighty-three there was a desire within the council to spread the good news about GLUE in Texas. The goddamn bible-est Bible Belt place there is. So they called in a reaper. 'Get me the Rhino' they said."

"Why'd they call him the Rhino?"

"That was his name."

"No...why was it his name?"

"I don't know. I guess he was horny. It's the least interesting thing about this story. Shut up."

"Sorry..."

"So then nobody hears anything from him for a couple of days. It's quiet, you know. He came in to town, saw the Council, left and then nothing.

"Next thing you know, it's on the news: there was a massacre in Texas. A gunman set fire to a church, and when the cops showed up he took out seventeen of them. Seventeen! Then he turns the gun on himself."

"The Rhino killed himself?"

"Shit no! Listen!"

"But you said..."

"I said he was an illusion master. He had a body handy, and he made it look just exactly the way he wanted it to look. No mess. No inquiries. Just a local tragedy in a small town that suddenly had no church in it. That made it ripe for the Principles of Transcending Bliss. Lo and behold, there was a representative of the Council there in a few hours, consoling everyone she could."

"All that to convert a small town?"

"No. One person."

"They targeted one person? Who?"

"Well, no. They targeted the whole town, but they only got one recruit. All of that was to convert this girl named Vivian Snelling. But their hope was of getting a toehold in Texas, and they got one."

"That's messed up."

"Listen, there's no limit to how far these folks will go to spread the word."

"Jesus. And this Rhino person, what happened to him?"

"I don't know. He did a lot of things for them back in the day. I have a whole dossier here if you're interested. He knows an awful lot about a bunch of assassinations. I can't imagine they want him to still be alive, so he's probably dead. Though I don't know if they have anyone good enough to take him out. Anyway, that's what I thought until I heard about this business up in Minnesota. It smells an awful lot like a Rhino. They sent someone after him, and he took care of them instead. Now there's an expert assassin somewhere out there hiding."

"What do you think they'll do next?"

"They'll call in a top tier reaper. The Llama or the Skunk."

"Those are code names?"

Esther sighed, "Yes those are code names."

"Tell me about them."

"The Skunk is a new player. He's been handling things on the east coast for a while. He's good in dense populations for some reason. He blends into a crowd I guess?"

"Okay."

"Much more likely is the Llama. She's experienced, and she's terrifying. Did you hear about the mixup in Texas with the politician's family in their car on the way to the gun range?"

"All dead without anyone reaching for a gun, no trace of who did it."

"It was the Llama."

"How do you know?"

"I have a source."

"Does your source think they'll send the Llama or the Skunk?"

"It doesn't work that way. When the bodies pile up, I'll know if GLUE is responsible."

"That's it?"

"No. When they have reapers die they let me know that too. That's how I heard about this Minnesota case."

"Okay so I'll need to find last known whereabouts of the Skunk and the Llama. Christ those names! This sounds like a children's book."

"Trust me it's not one. You need to find them, but they're looking for the Rhino. You need to find him first. Then they'll come to you."

"Okay, thanks Esther," Sarah said.

The church of the Generous Light of the Universe and Earth (GLUE) got its beginnings in 1962 in Clapford County, Indiana. A man named Osbert Solomon wrote a letter to the editor that was published in the Clapford Gazette. The letter was the prototype manifesto that espoused the virtue of going beyond mere bliss.

The idea was quite simple, really. It was a rejection of what Solomon perceived as the Hedonist bent of modern culture: merely pursuing pleasure was bound to lead to a fall for humanity, he thought.

The letter was fairly innocuous, unremarked by the inhabitants of south central Indiana, and would have been completely forgotten by time except that it was chanced upon by a college student digging through newspaper archives nearly ten years later in 1971. This student—Imogene Sneadly—was drugged out and finding deep prophetic meaning in the merest trivialities. She had been called a hedonist that very morning by her parents, and when she found that word in Solomon's letter, it resonated with her, and then re-resonated with her, and then re-resonated with her, until it formed an echo chamber, and she couldn't get it out of her mind. She decided to find Osbert Solomon and squeeze whatever wisdom she could out of him.

This was easy, an unassuming and quiet man, he had stayed right where he was in '62, still working for the same law firm, living much the same life.

Imogene had Osbert dictate a seven-step plan to go beyond bliss, which she happily typed up. However, because of the drugs and the mania, and the profoundly misguided view that Osbert was some sort of messianic figure full of occult wisdom (as opposed to a stodgy conservative law clerk who once wrote an unremarkable letter to a local newspaper) much was added in translation. And the resulting text was *The Principles of Transcending Bliss* that we all know today.

Imogene gave all the writing credit to Osbert, who was furious. He felt his reputation as a serious man was sullied. It would have been, had anyone in Indiana cared about this weird little book.

Instead practically nothing happened for a full year. The book passed through counterculture gatherings, concerts, festivals, campsites: hidden shadowy places out there unseen by most folks. Suddenly one day a "council" of people descended on Clapford County, rented some secluded land in the central part of the county, and set up a little compound. They claimed to be the experts in Osbert Solomon's philosophy and would honor his memory (laboring under the misapprehension that he had died).

Imogene Sneadly was thrilled and presented herself at the compound as the typist of the book, which the Council dismissed as impossible. There was only one name on the book, and it wasn't hers.

To prove she was the typist and belonged there, Imogene went and found Osbert Solomon and presented him at the gate. It was a bit of an over-calculation on her part. The Council was overjoyed at meeting Osbert, and held steady at no interest in Imogene Sneadly.

Likewise, Osbert Solomon had no interest in GLUE at all. It bore no resemblance to anything he'd ever thought or said, as far as he could see. He couldn't see a reason why anyone would want to stay. He said so, "If it were up to me, I'd be concerned about keeping people from leaving!"

The Council took this statement extremely seriously, since it came directly from the mouth of Osbert. They created the Reaper program: a group of assassins who would kill anyone who attempted to leave the organization. Later they would realize this also gave them options should critics need to be silenced.

The reapers gradually became a central feature of the organization, being the only statement heard directly from Osbert Solomon's mouth. In some members' eyes, transcending happiness was of secondary importance. Many members carried assault rifles at all times.

Techniques were developed, studied, and improved upon endlessly, tirelessly. They imported any strategy or technique they could find, and found flaws in them, and then fixed them. An elite force was formed unlike anything else.

The inevitable happened one day: a reaper decided to leave, believing himself to be capable of handling the entire squad alone. The results were catastrophically bloody.

After this point reapers were chosen from the lowest risk group. Only the most dedicated and best could be among them.

Still, an occasional reaper would try to leave. Every time they did, the outcome was horrific.

* _-*_ *

"The most important thing we have to do is find Dad," Lola said. The two were headed southwest towards Sioux Falls.

"We need to be smart about it, though. We don't want them to get to us. And we don't want them to follow us to him either."

"Yeah I hadn't even thought of that," she shuddered and looked out the window. There was little to see. The inky black of the night swallowed up everything at this hour. The window showed her the reflections from the lights of the dashboard. "I wish we could just call him. He never would get a cell phone though, while we were running from them."

"Good luck getting him to get one now."

"Where do you think he is?"

"Same as before. Sleeping in the woods. Off the map."

She shuddered again. "Are we even headed in the right direction?"

"We're avoiding the storm first."

"What? We're leaving him there?"

"No, he told me once he spent time in a place called Yankton. It's right on the river."

"So we think he'll be there?"

"Maybe. Or he'll head there."

"Okay," Lola said. She felt a little helpless, like this was all happening to her, and she had no agency in the proceedings.

"I was learning to be a reaper once," John said.

Lola's mouth dropped open, "I had no idea..."

"It's meant to be kept a secret. 'Do not disclose.' I didn't make it, there wasn't a need for two at the time, and I was always second best to the Llama."

She laughed, "The what? The llama? Were all the good names taken?"

"She picked it. I don't know why."

"Oh my god, what was yours?"

"Embarrassing. It's not the point right now. The Llama was intense, man. She had no feeling whatsoever. One time she killed another trainee—on accident, we thought— and asked if we could keep training anyway, or did we have to take the rest of the day off."

"What? How did she kill them? Knife or something?"

"A punch. She hits that hard that she killed a dude, and she still wanted to keep going."

"Jesus..."

"Anyway, she became a reaper, and there wasn't an opening for me. So I dropped off and went into strategy. Meanwhile she took on some dark ops, and she did some heinous things I don't even want to think about. Befton used to compare her to the Rhino."

"The Rhino?"

"Oh geez, a legendary reaper. One time he walked into a shopping mall in Pennsylvania full of people. He was the only one to walk out. Police suspected a gas leak, or some kind of chemical. That's how good he was. Massive production, no trace. None. Cops were chasing the air because no way a man did that."

"Okay, where is he now?" Lola asked.

John looked at her strangely, "Loose. Nobody's sure."

* _-*- *

Esther Cornwall took some personal time and drove to Yankton, South Dakota. It was a place she'd learned the Rhino had used to hide out before. She was, strictly speaking, off the field assignment for the Minnesota case, but she had a feeling about this place, and she wanted to check it out. She couldn't officially work the case, but they couldn't tell her she couldn't go there in her free time, she thought.

Of all the places she knew the Rhino used for hideouts, this was the closest to the incident in Minnesota. The fact that information was known to her meant it was likely known to others within GLUE. That made it a known "unusable" hideout. If that was true and GLUE thought so too, they might not even bother looking this way until all else failed, which made it perfect.

The actual structure where the hideout stood was west of town in a small wooded area. It was a little shack with a bed and a table inside. There was a wood stove and a charcoal grill. No electricity, no running water.

Esther visited the building, but saw no sign that anyone had been there in some time. That didn't mean he wasn't coming, she reasoned. She decided to spend a couple days in town and keep coming back to check for life in the old shack.

On the third day, she saw two young people walking around. She knew they were too young to be doing hits in the eighties, but who were these two?

She moved in a little closer, within earshot. She could hear that they were talking but couldn't make any of it out. Then the woman turned enough that she could see her face and she recognized her immediately.

"Lola and John!" Esther said stepping into view.

John scrutinized her for a second, "You're not GLUE," he said, "Who are you?"

"I'm a student," she said.

"You're a little old to be a student," John said.

"Watch your damn mouth," she responded.

"How do you know our names?" Lola asked.

She showed them her badge, "I'm Esther Cornwall. I've been studying you for a long time."

"We didn't do it. We were supposed to stay in Minnesota I know, but we're trying to find him here," John said. He was nervous now that he'd seen that badge.

"I'm here to find him too," Esther said.

"You're looking for my dad?"

"Yes, obviously they're after him. He's the key to all this. I want to know what he knows. It's the reason they're after him isn't it?"

"I thought it was because you aren't supposed to leave," Lola said.

"The council doesn't let anybody leave," said John.

"Surely some folks get away without being chased down by five assassins."

"I...I don't even know," said Lola, "I don't know if people get out. People have left before, and then we never see them again. That's all I know."

"Obviously your father is a special case."

"I don't see why...?"

"Your dad is the Rhino. He's—"

"He's WHAT?"

"The Rhino. An assassin for GLUE. You didn't know?"

"I didn't know. John just told me about the Rhino when we were driving down here. But he didn't know who it was."

"Well..." he said.

"Did you...know it was my dad?"

"Umm, yes. I did. He told me a long time ago because he knew I was a trainee."

"But he couldn't tell me?"

"You weren't supposed to find out. The less you know the safer you are."

"I'm sorry," Esther said, "I shouldn't have said anything. I assumed you knew after being on the run for so long."

"Well...What's done is done," Lola said sarcastically, "We might as well move forward now that I know my dad is a professional murderer and hid it from me my entire life."

"I am so sorry you had to find out from me. I just came here, like I said, because I want to know what he knows that they're willing to kill to keep from getting out."

"God and I forgot they're trying to kill him."

"And us," added John.

"Oh right and us," she said grimly.

"It's not all bad news. Your dad is the best at what he does. They've been trying to get to him. They've sent pros. They sent five at once the other day. All of this, and he's not got a scratch on him."

"They'll escalate," John said.

"My fear as well," Esther said, "I expect the Llama or the Skunk will be involved before long."

"Jesus," said John.

"Anyway, what did you say your name was?"

"Esther."

"Esther, it's not what he knows that's dangerous. It's what he wants."

"What he wants?"

"He wants to be free. He'll never be free, none of us will, as long as the Council exists—as long as GLUE exists."

"He wants to take them down," Esther said.

"Correct," Lola said.

"Then I have to help him do it," said Esther. She took a business card from her pocket and handed it to Lola. "I have to go back to Chicago in a couple days. I am not officially working this case. But I can help. Tell him I can help."

"I don't think he'll trust you."

"I know," she said.

*_-*_ *

Sarah Navarro arrived at the crime scene in Minnesota that afternoon. State police were very concerned about the presence of a federal agent.

"This is your investigation," she told them, "I'm not claiming jurisdiction. Not at this time anyway. The incident that took place here may connect with an ongoing federal investigation. If we find that it does in fact, we will need to have a conversation at that point."

This did not make the state police any less nervous. She got the lay of the land, a few salient facts and then left them.

She walked down the road away from the cabin. She went out the lane where Lola and John had seen the reapers come out of the woods. She looked into the woods to see if she could spot Any sign that someone had stopped there.

"Can I help you?" a woman asked. Sarah turned to look at her. She was in her twenties or thirties, dressed in a teal wind suit, with curlers in her hair and dark, thick-rimmed sunglasses on.

"Hello. I'm just looking at these trees here," Sarah said.

"I see. Are you involved in the investigation?" the stranger asked.

"I am not, as a matter of fact."

"You're a federal agent," the woman said pointing at the identification badge on Sarah's lanyard.

"Yes well, believe it or not there is more than one case being pursued in the world at a given time."

"So you wouldn't be interested in seeing the shack in the woods that was built by the guy who lived there?" she pointed down the lane.

"I...hmmm. I may..." she said.

The stranger smiled, "I'll take you there."

Lola and John hated the shack. It was uncomfortable and hot. There were insects and vermin. They couldn't bathe. It wasn't clear they even needed to be there. There was only a slim chance Lola's father would come this way. And even if he did, would it matter if they were sleeping somewhere more comfortable?

The shack did offer them an opportunity to think about what to do next without having to worry about being found. Although the lady from the government came straight there, and that wasn't a good sign.

Lola was still adjusting to this. They'd been fleeing GLUE for a long time before settling in Minnesota when they thought they were safe. Adjusting and staying vigilant were part of her life now, but her father being a reaper and not telling her about it; that was a new level on which to practice her flexibility.

Then this woman recognized both of them on sight. How did she do that? She said it because she was a fed agent and she'd studied them. Why was she studying them?

The agent's presence did seem to corroborate their hunch that her dad would come this way. Among the many questions and worries swirling around her was "What if we're in completely the wrong place?" Lola had no better guess about where to find her father than either the agent or John had. There was just something arbitrary about this choice and it worried her. It bothered her that his own daughter didn't know where to go.

They did not see Esther again for two days, but they assumed they were under constant surveillance and they felt her gaze at all times. It was another reason to hate this place, Lola thought.

The third day Esther came back, knocked on the door and John let her in.

"There have been some developments you need to be aware of," she said.

"First, the field agent assigned to your father's disappearance was killed in Minnesota."

"The Llama..." said John.

"Unlikely," said Esther, "It's wasted motion: the death of this agent didn't need to happen for her to find her quarry, but it does bring heavy attention from an entire federal organization. We get mad as hornets when one of our own goes down, and we're pissed right now. Why would she bring that kind of heat on herself? Why poke the hornets nest? It makes no sense."

"I know her," John said.

"You what?"

"It's a long story. Anyway, this is her. She's raising the stakes because it makes the kill more impressive."

"Don't say kill," said Lola, "I can't...I can't." She looked at him with a face full of fear.

"The task then. There's the best ever she's going after, which ought to be enough, but luck could be involved if she, umm, completed the task. On the other hand if she pulls it off under the gaze of every agent in America, she becomes a legend."

"That's stupid," said Lola.

"And reckless," said Esther, "it doesn't sound like any reaper I've ever heard of."

"It's her, trust me."

"Well her or not, the field agent assigned to your case is dead. They've asked me to go into the field now. I'm the agent assigned to this case."

"Okay?" said Lola.

"They want to know why I'm in South Dakota."

"What did you tell them?" John asked.

"I'm investigating a lead. The point is, you can't stay in this shack. It's marked now, so move on before you get caught."

"But where should we go?" asked Lola.

"Don't tell me. It's better if I don't know."

"Okay, we won't tell you," said John, "Where are you going?"

"Obviously I can't tell you that."

"Okay, well good luck," said Lola, sensing the conversation was at an impasse.

"Yes, good luck. I'm sure we'll meet again."

Esther left them to fend for themselves. She had to report to the crime scene in Minnesota first thing the next morning.

"It's convenient you're already in South Dakota," her superior had said, "Why are you in South Dakota?"

She knew better than to ask how he knew where she was. She simply drove up to the cabin and reported at 8 am.

Another agent met her there. She didn't recognize him, but he waved to her when she walked up and beckoned to her to come on over.

"Good morning Agent Cornwall," he said, "I'm Jeremiah Thompson. I'm handling the death of Agent Navarro. It's related to your case since she was here investigating it, right?"

"Nice to meet you," she said, "They're very much related. Although I don't think we're looking for the same fella."

"A woman," he said.

"Excuse me?" she asked.

"I'm looking for a woman. Lavender wind suit, according to the video."

Esther immediately connected the dots and was very excited, "Jesus, you have her on video?"

"The suspect?"

"The Llama," she said in awe.

"Llama?" he was very lost.

"We need to talk," she said, "I know where they're headed. Both of them, they're both headed to Indiana. My rhino and your llama."

"Rhino?" he said. Esther was already walking to her car, "Wait a minute!" he yelled after her.

"In the car!" she demanded and climbed into the driver's seat.

Jeremiah shrugged to no one and walked over to Esther's passenger door and got in.

"Look we're not leaving yet, there's a whole mountain of work to do here," Jeremiah said.

"I know that. We don't need to tell the local police all our business though. Hence the car."

"Oh," he said, embarrassed.

"I want to see your crime scene too. And mine. But first I have to tell you everything about a weird cult based out of Indiana called GLUE."

She explained it all to him: the history, the reaper program, and how now the best reaper in history was being pursued by someone who wanted to prove their own excellence.

"She killed Navarro so that we would all come after her. Imagine taking down the best assassin ever with the best agents in the world after you as well, and then getting away. It's the stuff of legend."

"I don't know if we're the best agents in the world..." Jeremiah trailed off.

"Okay maybe we're a couple of duds. She doesn't know that."

"Hey! I'm not a dud."

"I know we're the best. Never doubt it again."

Jeremiah was confused, "I'm confused," he said.

"It doesn't matter. He's going to shut them down for good. That's his plan. To do that, he has to go to their headquarters in Indiana. There will be a lot of bloodshed. But if he isn't successful, there will be more."

"So we have to help an illegal assassin?"

"He just wants to be free. And it stops all of this. Hundreds of parents will find out where their kids have been, and communities will stop being terrorized."

"I just want to get Navarro's killer."

"She's headed to the same place. We're all headed to the same finale."

"She needs to be brought to justice, before a judge. Not in a cornfield."

"Agreed."

"All right, let's check out your lead."

Mathias Befton was concerned and he voiced his concerns at the next Council meeting. Already he'd had an operation go sideways in Minnesota, and now the reaper he sent in to clean up the mess decided to take out a federal agent instead of handling the Rhino.

He had spent the past couple of days trying to make contact with the Skunk, who would be the next reaper in line to deal with the mess, but he was having no luck.

Rhee Stancroft and the rest of the Council were not pleased. Above all, their organization was predicated on having no loose ends, and suddenly there were loose ends everywhere: the Rhino, his daughter and son-in-law, the Llama, and the Skunk. On top of this, feds were going to be sniffing around, and the reaper program was running dangerously low on bench strength.

Rhee viewed this as a failure on the part of Mathias in no uncertain terms. The Council was inclined to agree. There was a motion on the table to remove Mathias from the Council. Perhaps from the organization and this plane of existence, if a reaper could be found to do it.

"I accept the judgment of this Council, of course," he said, his voice echoing throughout the hall, "but you need to be warned: the Rhino isn't going to rest again. He knows he will never be free so long as we are here."

"So he will live in hiding forever."

"No. He is a cornered predator. He was willing to live in hiding before, but we went after him. Now he will come after us."

"The Llama is out there. The Skunk is out there. We are prepared for this contingency are we not?" Rhee asked.

"I do not know," Mathias said, and crumpled into his chair.

"Council members, this is incompetence," she said, "we can't even say the state of our readiness at this time, because we've entrusted everything to this man who was unworthy of our trust."

A vote was held. It was heavily against Mathias staying in the Council. He just stared straight ahead and said nothing as the Council moved on to other business.

His temples throbbed. He couldn't see anything but the point in front of him he'd chosen to fix his eyes on. They'd let him keep his life. That was something, he thought, though that was subject to change. *Likely not a subject they'd discuss with me in the room*, he thought, *More of the world.*

A messenger came into the room and left a sheet of paper in front of him. It said "SKUNK IS DEAD. BODY FOUND IN NEVADA."

The news didn't shake him out of his shock and numbness at first. His first thought was that it was someone else's problem now. None of his concern. The message wouldn't even have come to him had the outcome of the vote been known outside the room.

There was some mystery to be solved here: how did this happen? Nothing more. The timing was unfortunate for GLUE with the Rhino probably bearing down on them. That was all that interested him about the note.

But something didn't feel right about it. He read it again and again. It gave him something else to fixate in besides the meeting.

"Nevada!" he said out loud.

The meeting stopped. A Council member was mid speech and stopped speaking to turn to Mathias.

He felt he'd better explain.

"I received communication just now that the Skunk is dead."

"What does this have to do with Nevada?" the angry interrupted Council member asked.

"He was found there."

"And...?"

"He took care of the east coast for us."

"So he was in the wrong place and he died?" Rhee asked.

"He was. But why was he in the wrong place?"

"I don't know, do you?"

"I don't but I will find out for you," he said, standing from his chair and heading for the door.

"Please don't!" Rhee called after him.

"Too late," he said slapping the door on his way out.

* _-*-_ *

John and Lola thought about where to head next. The first thing to decide was again whether to try to meet up with Lola's dad, and risk leading the Llama straight to him, or to head elsewhere and try to lead the Llama on a wild goose chase, potentially saving her father's life.

They decided to confront the problem head-on with her father. There was no guarantee they were being followed. The only way they could be of any use was to charge in and take the risk.

They passed through Omaha, Kansas City, and St. Louis and headed east across Illinois into southern Indiana.

"This is a long way to go," Lola said.

"We're almost there."

"How do we do this?" Lola asked.

"How do we do what?"

"Whatever comes next. We charge in? That's what you said last night. We just drive straight in to the compound and take it from there?"

"Well...no I guess not. We should probably get the lay of the land first."

"How will we do that?"

"There's a ridge north of the compound. It will give us a good view of everything. If I'm right if your dad is headed to the compound, he'll go there too. It's the best spot."

"And the Llama? Wouldn't she go there too, if it's such a good spot?"

"I don't know."

"I don't like 'I don't know.'"

"I know. Do you think I do? We're gambling here on the whole thing. After all this time fleeing reapers, we're running straight at them. Just because we think your dad is doing the same. If we're wrong and he's not, we're dead. If we're right we're still probably dead. We have to fight their whole militia," he trailed off. The odds seemed to be piling up against them the more he talked, "I don't know. I'm half hoping we can meet your dad and convince him to run. Hell even if we see him it might be too late for us. What we're doing is risky—deadly risky—but I can't see any other way."

Lola sighed and stared out the window at the trees, "I agree," she said, "We have a plan. We'll head for a hill and see what there is to see."

The ridge north of the compound could only be approached on foot by a quarter-mile walk through the woods. Once arrived, a person would not be greeted by a breathtaking view of the valley. All around them would be maple leaves, oak leaves, etc. that would block ones view more than a few meters in front of their face.

To gain the lookout perspective, a person needed to either climb a tree or shove some branches out of the way.

On arriving at the ridge, John tested his luck at both approaches. Climbing a tree was harder than he remembered from childhood. It was also noisy, he thought. The whole tree shook when he moved, all the leaves rustled, and the weight of wanting very badly not to be discovered made those rustles sound extremely conspicuous.

Besides this, once in the tree, he thought he would be in a poor defensive or offensive position should someone else arrive on the scene. More importantly, it left Lola vulnerable.

He abandoned the climb.

The two of them started moving branches out of the way to see what kind of view they could get. They were hard at work doing this for several minutes before they heard a voice say, "Stop what you're doing! You're coming with us!"

They turned around very slowly to find they'd been caught by two GLUE sentries who were patrolling the ridge in case the Rhino showed up. They had assault rifles trained on Lola and John.

"After all this, we get caught playing in the trees," Lola said.

"Quiet!" a sentry said, "We're taking you to the Council."

"Do you know who I am?" another mystery voice said from above them.

A man jumped down from a low branch on a tree behind the sentries. They turned to face him. "The Rhino," the second sentry said in awe.

"Dad!" said Lola.

"Do you know what I am capable of?" he asked.

The two sentries glanced at one another and nodded. They both laid down their guns and sat down on the ground.

"And do you know who I am and what I'm capable of?" a woman's voice said from behind a tree behind the Rhino.

The Llama stepped into view, and everyone froze.

"Llama," John said.

"Beetle," she said in return.

"Beetle?" Lola looked at him.

"I told you it was embarrassing."

The two sentries began to realize they were in the clear now, and started to stand and reach for their guns.

"Hold on there," said the Llama. They stopped.

"What do you want?" Rhino asked.

"Same as you partner," she said, "I want out."

Lola looked at her in total surprise.

"There's no getting out as long as GLUE exists," Rhino said.

"Precisely," she responded, "You, me, Beetle, and your little girl are going to walk down there and put an end to all of it. Then, we can be free."

"How do you propose to do that?" John asked.

"Threats and intimidation, dummy," she said, "and a little help from the federal government."

"The feds?" Rhino said.

"Yes. I killed one to keep them on my trail. They want this place shut down too, only they've never had a good reason to do it til now."

"That's insane," John said.

"Why? They're not going to let me be when this all collapses anyway. We just need to make it count. Make it worth it. Set these people free."

Lola looked down in the direction of the compound. Leaves blocked her view. She hadn't thought about this ordeal as benefitting anyone but herself and her family until now.

"What is our plan?" John said.

"We need to get to the Council," Rhino said.

"And it would be nice if we got there without having to fight anyone," Llama said.

John thought about that for a second, "Where is the Skunk?"

"We don't need to worry about him," the Llama said pointedly.

Rhino turned sharply to face her in amazement, "Did you..?"

She nodded.

"Without him," John continued, "this is a little bit less complicated. What if we're your prisoners, and you need to take us to see the Council?"

"Why am I doing this? It's not how we do things," Llama said.

"You found us right here. You didn't want to kill us right outside the compound. It would raise questions."

"Not the way I do it," she said.

"It doesn't have to be air tight," John said, "We just need to get in the gate."

"And then what?" Lola asked. She'd been standing quietly feeling disconnected from what was happening, "We need to be sure we finish this. Our lives depend on what we do. Not just our lives, but everyone down there. It has to go right. For them."

"We'll get it right," John said.

Esther and Jeremiah were in Esther's car a few dozen yards away from the gate to the GLUE compound. The gate itself was an unimpressive thing: a red metal tubed farm gate. It would have been more at home keeping cattle in than in keep federal agents out. On either side of the gate, however, there stood three guards armed with AK-47s. The guards were malnourished, gaunt specimens in t shirts and jeans that were too large for them in both directions.

They were watching the strangers in the car uneasily. Jeremiah was concerned about this but Esther did not mind.

"Whatever they're about to do, we're creating a diversion. These people have their attention on us, not the perimeter."

"What makes you think they're going to sneak in through the perimeter?"

"Well, I don't have a good answer for that," she confessed, "I just can't imagine them walking in through the front gate with all this heat on them."

"There they are," Jeremiah pointed. He was right. A woman Esther recognized as the Llama was walking behind Lola and John and the Rhino. She was accompanied by two other guards.

"There's your killer," she said.

"Wait which one?"

"The one who has them all captured."

He considered his next steps, "We need support," he said.

"We do. Call it in."

The six walked up to the gate, nervous. The guards at the gate were equally nervous. A reaper bringing in her quarry alive was unheard of. They recognized this particular quarry of course. The Rhino was in front of them, which increased the stakes somewhat. Without a protocol to follow, they stalled for time to catch their breath and radio to the central building for guidance.

The folks in the central building were similarly confused about what to do. "Let us get Mathias Befton," they said.

"They're not getting in," said Esther.

"Back up is en route, but we are in the middle of nowhere. So it might be a little while."

"We can help them," she said.

"The back up?"

"Them!" she said, pointing at the gate.

"How?"

"Follow my lead," she said as she opened her car door and got out.

The guards at the gate got animated at this point. Two federal agents wearing the blue jackets with yellow lettering had just emerged from the car they'd been eyeing suspiciously for the past hour. They radioed in to Mathias that this had occurred.

"What do they want?" the answer crackled back.

"Can we help you?" a guard yelled at the two advancing agents.

"This woman," Esther gestured, "known as the Llama is wanted for questioning in connection with a federal investigation."

Lola looked at Esther. Esther winked at her.

The guards radioed back to Mathias, "They want to speak to the Llama."

"Absolutely not!" hissed the radio, "Get them inside the compound! Now!"

"You're going to need a warrant," the guard yelled back at Esther.

"Suits me," she yelled back.

"What's happening?" Jeremiah asked her.

"We don't do anything til your back up gets here. In the meantime, they have a plan, and we helped them act it out."

"What plan do they have?"

"I don't know," she said, and turned to walk back to the car.

The Llama and the two sentries from the woods marched the Rhino and Lola and John to the Council Hall.

The Council was there waiting for them. Mathias Befton was there as well.

"We heard you were here," Mathias said, "Why have you brought them here? Why have you brought the feds here?"

In one smooth motion, the Llama and the two sentries passed weapons to their prisoners and all six people held weapons aimed at members of the Council.

"You disband GLUE now, or else," the Llama yelled.

"You'll never make it out of here alive," Mathias said, "The whole place is full of people carrying guns."

Lola stepped forward, "We have made contact with federal agents. They are waiting outside to take you down."

The Llama looked at her strangely.

"You are bluffing," said Mathias.

"No she's not," said a voice from the doorway. Everyone turned to see Esther Cornwall and Jeremiah Thompson standing in the doorway, "Every single Council member here is under arrest."

Rhee Stancroft laughed, "You won't be arresting us. Just like these sad fools, you won't be making it out of the compound alive."

"That's adorable Rhee," said Esther, "threatening me like this after our backup arrived and we have arrested everyone in the compound. No one is going to defend you. You're coming with me."

"You're lying."

"Come and see for yourself."

"Fine. I will," said Rhee. She walked out the door, and out of curiosity, everyone followed her.

The entire GLUE compound was covered with National Guard. Every member of the organization had thrown down their gun and gone to stand in a big mass outside the Council Hall. They did it willingly.

The Llama walked up to Jeremiah and stuck her arms out, "I'm turning myself in," she said.

All of the Council members knelt on the ground and cooperated. The threat was over, GLUE was effectively no more.

Lola and John were allowed to go free after answering a few questions, as was most of the liberated GLUE population. Anyone in a position of power, or who could be linked to criminal wrongdoing was detained, arrested, and charged.

It came out that in addition to killing any members that attempted to leave, the reapers were available for hire. Because of this GLUE had a number of connections to organized crime that were of interest to several other federal investigations.

The Llama cooperated with these investigations as did the Rhino. Rhino was given consideration for this when it came to charging and sentencing. He got five years.

The Llama was not so lucky. She had killed a federal agent knowingly. It didn't matter how helpful she was, prosecutors were out for blood. All of this she bore happily, understanding that these were happier consequences than killing indefinitely lest she be killed herself. She was more than happy to assist with any investigation that put the Council members away for good.

The canoe at Lola's father's place in Minnesota saw a lot of use that summer. They learned to balance in the boat pretty quickly. Eventually they stopped scanning the shoreline for anyone who might be watching them.

Lucius Stancroft

Harvey Applegate stood at his living room picture window and watched a black Cadillac kick up dust as it came up his gravel driveway. The car pulled up near the house and parked. The rock dust scattered with the wind across the Applegate's front yard. Harvey set a glass of iced tea down on an end table and stepped out onto the front porch.

Harvey recognized the man who got out of the car. The man was awkwardly dressed in clothes meant to make him look like he fit in, to make him appear casual and relatable. He was wearing blue jeans that were noticeably crisp and un-broken-in, a polo shirt with Deccrin Seed Company branding stitched in, and a clean, stiff canvas work jacket overtop, also embroidered with the Deccrin logo.

"You know I can't buy from you, Lucius," said Harvey as the man stepped up to the porch.

"Harvey! How are you?"

"Well, Lucius, I guess I'm doing fine. Headed out this afternoon to finish up planting beans. You're too late again this year."

"Come on, Harvey, I know what time of year it is. This ain't a sales call. I'm just stopping in to see how you've been."

"Okay then, why are you wearing that costume?"

Lucius chuckled, "I guess you never know, maybe Dekart gave up on you after last year and you needed to place an order. What kind of friend would I be if I wasn't ready to step in and help?"

Harvey reacted to this uneasily. Lucius felt he may have overstepped.

"How *was* your year last year?" he asked.

"Fine, I guess. Rain didn't let us down. We came out all right in the end."

Lucius realized what had made Harvey uncomfortable wasn't the insinuation he'd had a bad year.

"Well, listen Harvey, I don't want to take up too much of your time..."

"Why do you come out here every year, Lucius?"

"I'm sorry?"

"You're in the business, you know damn well that by January, everyone around here is pretty much fixed."

"Like I said, I just come by to say Hi."

"Like you said. And like I said, why do you do it?"

"I don't know, just neighborly I suppose. I'm not here all fall and winter, I just miss folks I guess."

"Neighborly, huh? Is it neighborly for that uncle of yours to be trying to foreclose on my land?"

"What?"

"Just cause he read somewhere it's going to be dry. Hasn't even been dry yet, it just might be, and he's already got plans drawn up for a subdivision right over there," he pointed at an empty field next to the house.

"Listen what my uncle does—"

"I know, I know. Not connected, none of your business. You're just circling like vultures. Both of you. And I've got a damn hard season ahead of me if it is going to be dry. Last thing I need right now is you two Stancrofts licking their chops, hoping I fail."

"I'm awful sorry, Harvey. I'd better go."

"You'd better, " he repeated, "that'd be the neighborly thing to do."

In the spring, as the trees erupt into green and the birds return, planting begins in the fields of Clapford County as it does most places. Seed must be sold, orders are placed, deliveries are made. There is an entire infrastructure behind providing the seeds to be planted to move agriculture forward.

For most of the farms, it's too late for seed salesmen. They've got arrangements with big seed companies all lined out and there's no changing course. Not during the planting season.

"Come back this winter," they'd say. But by winter they'd be well into the pocket of whichever company got to them in the fall.

Lucius Stancroft was a seed salesman. He was fantastically successful out west in Illinois, Iowa, Missouri, and Kansas, it was said. Folks knew he spent his falls and winters there and just missed the local sales by the time he came back home.

But home he came, every spring, with the robins and the maple leaves. He'd make the rounds to all the farms, even the ones where the seed was already in the ground.

They'd tell him no. He didn't seem to care. He had an easy manner when he went on a sales call. He'd say "of course you've got yourself all lined out. You don't have to buy from me. How'd your crops do last year?" And the farmers would talk about their yield, and he'd listen and act like he gave a damn.

After this he'd come home to his lonely two-bedroom East of Hardy. He stayed out of town as much as he could. He made a habit of quietly arriving in town and quietly leaving so he never had to see his uncle Oliver Stancroft.

Oliver has long held the opinion that seed sales were beneath the dignity of the Stancroft clan, and made sure to say so whenever he saw Lucius. Though, he'd only come to his realization about the profession when Lucius first announced it one Thanksgiving.

At the time, Oliver had been deep in the throes of a plan to "save" the family name. And it certainly did him no favors to have his nephew traipsing from farm to farm around the locals, demonstrating to them that one from such a family could descend to such a lowly state: hobnobbing with common folk..

Lucius didn't exactly hate his uncle, but he did feel it was best if they never crossed paths. He volunteered for the west central region to be away from home during the family-visit-heavy holiday season. So after an initial round of visits to the local farms, he'd more or less stick to his home for the spring and early summer. From there he could call all of his clients and check on their year, without making himself too noticeable in town. He even drove to the next town over to buy groceries. Folks there knew who he was, of course, but they weren't expecting the grand show of dignity he felt the people of Hardy were expecting from him.

The facts of Lucius' situation were truly that he made his money elsewhere during the fall and winter. Oliver had spread a story to save face, but it was partially true, although he had greatly exaggerated the extent to which Lucius was successful.

Lucius was actually worried he would lose his home. One more bad year selling seed and he would have to change course. The facts were undeniable. Admitting it to himself was easy enough. Admitting it in earshot of his uncle was another thing altogether. He dreaded to think he might have to inquire about work at some point in the near future, perhaps even from Oliver.

There was a great deal of the Stancroft pride in Lucius. He dared not admit he was wrong, and less so that his uncle may have been right. It was easier to him to say the job is great and he was not good at it than to say the job may have had limited opportunities.

A new company out of Oklahoma—Snzl—was seducing clients with technology, innovation, and dazzle. That was that.

That summer was one of the driest ever on record. As Lucius called to check in on his clients out west, more and more complained, "Listen Lucius, this summer's been real dry and I don't have hardly any yield. But Jones up the road has plenty of beans coming in. She's not getting any more rain than me, it's those Snzl seeds. They grow anywhere, no matter how dry it is. I'm sorry man, I can't use Deccrin again next year if it won't grow. It's nothing personal. I've been buying from you for years. I just have to protect my farm."

"Is there anything I can do to change your mind?"

"Make beans grow in dry ground, I guess, but somebody else already did that. You could do it cheaper, maybe."

The more phone calls Lucius made, the more he realized his book of business was becoming depleted, and he wouldn't make enough in sales to even cover his travel in the fall. He decided to call his regional manager, Trent.

Trent worked in the company's corporate headquarters in Chicago on a team with a dozen other regional sales managers. He gave his front line sales associates a lot of freedom to do whatever needed to be done, and in turn he didn't expect to be brought day to day problems. Lucius hated to call and ask for anything. The answer was invariably "I trust you to solve this yourself," which Lucius thought was empowering sometimes, but on the occasions he really needed help or advice it was frustratingly useless.

Nevertheless, Lucius made the call.

A woman's voice answered, "Hello?"

"Hi, this is Lucius Stancroft. I'm trying to get ahold of Trent."

"Trent?" The voice asked. It sounded familiar but Lucius couldn't place it.

"Trent Olbermeier, he's a regional manager."

"Yes, umm, what did you say your name was? Luke?"

"Lucius..."

"Yes, Luke, I know who Trent is. Were you on his team?"

"I...am...on his team?"

"No Luke, you're not. You should have heard before now. I let Trent go," the voice's familiarity made sense now. Lucius was talking to the CEO, Veronica Hallstaff.

"Oh my, you let him go? What happened?"

"What do you mean what happened? We're getting killed out there. GMO's during a drought. They grow. Our seeds don't. I had to cut corporate staff in half to stay afloat."

"Yikes!"

"You're commission only, right?"

"Uhh, yeah," he said.

"Good. We can't afford to have all these people in the field if we're paying them to be out there. You bring in money, you get paid. Simple. Clean. I love it."

"Sure, but..."

"What were you going to ask Trent?"

"Well, I've been keeping up with my clients out west: making phone calls, seeing how they're doing."

"Good."

"They're all dropping me next year and going with Snzl."

There was a long pause before Veronica spoke, "So you're not bringing in any money either, Torncraft?"

"Not none, no. I said 'all,' it's not really all. But the thing is, I don't make enough on the sales I have left out there to be able to afford to go out there and sell."

"That's not a question."

"What are we doing, Veronica...for next year....or for the year after, to compete? I just need to know that, we might not have the science down right now, but we will, and when we do, we'll be competitive again."

"We're praying it rains again."

"What?"

"There's no R&D. No science, no GMOs coming. We don't have the budget for any of that. We're having a bad year because it didn't rain. That's all. So our strategy is pray for rain."

Lucius took a long time to respond. He was breathing heavy and his ears felt hot, "I quit," he said.

Veronica didn't respond before Lucius hung up.

"I understand," she said. It was for no one's benefit. She hung up the phone.

Lucius braced himself for what inevitably came next. He would have to call his uncle to ask for a job. Everything in him revolted against this idea. It ran directly counter to his strategy of avoiding at all cost.

He tried applying anywhere else he could think of. The economy was slowing down in Clapford County and the outside world. There was nothing out there that they couldn't hire someone else for cheaper.

The Stancroft family bank might not have much need for someone right now, but Oliver would hire Lucius anyway. He would lose money to protect the family name. More than likely he'd fire someone else to give Lucius a job.

That was corporate favoritism and completely reprehensible, but he'd do it just the same.

Lucius knew it.

He made the call.

"Hello?" Oliver said.

"Hi Uncle Oliver. It's Lucius."

"Oh, hi Lucius," he said flatly.

"How are you?" Lucius asked.

"I'm doing fine, and you?"

"Ehhh well..." he started.

"I knew it!" Oliver said.

"What?"

"It was only a matter of time. Seed sales aren't good enough for you are they? Like I said all along. It's beneath you."

"Whether it is or not is neither here nor there. The company's folding and nobody's going to have a job next year."

"Hmm. Rough year," Oliver said.

"I was wondering if you have anything at the bank I could do."

Oliver sighed heavily, "I'm not running a charity, Lucius. Times are tough here too. Everyone's tightening their belts and making do with less these days. I can't just add staff on a whim."

That knocked Lucius sideways. For the next several seconds he felt like he'd been thrown in the deep end of a swimming pool. He couldn't really see and he couldn't really hear.

He got off the phone on auto-pilot saying, "Thank you Uncle Oliver I'll talk to you soon." He wasn't even sure he didn't cut his uncle off mid-sentence. He was in a state of shock.

He had never seriously felt like his livelihood was in any jeopardy because he always knew the bank would be there to take him in if he needed it to be there. Now it wasn't going to be there, and he was going to have to figure something out. It was a completely normal contingency for everyone else, but for Lucius an entirely unthought-of contingency. He felt guilty about having just expected the job to be there for him. He thought he might need to seriously re-examine somethings about his life.

His phone rang and his answered it, "Hello?"

"Did I get ya?" Oliver said.

"What?" Lucius was not comprehending much of anything anyway, let alone following the logic of what his uncle was saying.

"Ha ha! I did get you!"

"I'm not following. This was a joke?"

"Of course it's a joke, dummy. Come in on Monday, and we'll do a formal interview. I gotta see your C. V. to know what you've been doing so I can figure out how you can help me. But trust me, I'll figure something out."

"Okay," Lucius said numbly and hung up the phone.

Lucius showed up to the bank Monday morning in a sharp navy suit, bright blue tie and a clean shave. Even if the job was being handed to him, he still wanted to be in the habit of making an effort. He hoped one day he'd need to make one again.

Oliver ushered him in to his office and asked to see his C. V. He read through it very carefully, shook his head, and appeared to read it again. This time he held it a little closer to his face as if it would change the words.

"I don't know what I expected. You were a field salesman."

"Correct," Lucius said, stressing the formality of his tone.

"You went to farms?"

"Correct."

"You built relationships with farmers?"

"Correct."

"Hmm," Oliver said. He seemed to have a need to mull that over for moment, "Did you ever go out and meet with any of the farmers around here?"

"Yes."

"Trying to sell them seeds?"

"Not really. Of course I would have been open to selling to any of them, but I knew they were set up long before they talked to me. I just wanted them to see my face every year and build some trust. You never know when it might pay off down the line."

"Tell me about why you left Deccrin."

"It's been a rough year of course. There's no rain. Crops aren't growing as well. A lot of my clients are making the move to GMOs next year, ones that grow well in drier soil. It's kind of an insurance policy for them."

"So you have a bad year and you quit?"

"Well no, I wanted to fight to get them back. But I didn't want to feed them a lot of nonsense. They know when you're not being honest with them. So I wanted to be able to at least say we'd have seeds like that in the future: that we had a plan for them. I called up to ask what our plan was, and there was no plan. So I quit."

"Ah," Oliver said, "Well, here at home it hasn't been any easier. It's been a bad growing year and it's coming at a real bad time for lot of folks out there from a financial perspective. There are some farmers who were on the verge of losing their farms to us last year, before all this drought. Then this year hits and..." he trailed off, letting Lucius do the work for himself.

"You're going to foreclose on people's farms?"

"The bank is. We don't have much choice, Lucius. There are shareholders to consider. If we give these people another year of grace period, what then? Do we expect them to turn it around?"

"But you can't just foreclose on them!"

"It's not like it's happening out of the blue. They know what their situation is. They're probably already packing. Besides, I'm not foreclosing on them. You are."

"I am?"

"Yes. If you want a job here at the bank, I need you to use those relationships you built with these farmers and resolve these situations for me."

"Suppose I can resolve the situation without foreclosing?"

"I don't see how, but if you can do that and everyone's happy, go right ahead."

The dry summer's impact rippled through the town's economy. Less money came in from the harvest, less money was spent bringing in the harvest, fewer farm hand jobs, less gas sold, less wear and tear on farm implements meant fewer sales and repairs, fewer farm hands meant the high schoolers who would normally be out working were staying at home, not making money, not spending money. Teenagers didn't go on as many dates. Fewer movie tickets sold. Less clothes were bought.

Everywhere business went down, so did the number of man hours they needed to do the work. Cascading into even less money flowing through town.

Through the dry weeks that piled up one on top of another, Lucius researched the situations of each of the farmers facing tough decisions in the fall. He looked at their paperwork, drove out and checked out their land, made phone calls. He worked out to the penny, for every single one of them, what their exact financial position was. How far behind they were, how much further behind they were projected to be, even after the coming harvest.

The situation was bleak. The logic that led to foreclosure seemed inescapable. He began to fear the fall, for the heartaches he'd signed up to bring to all of these families.

As he looked at all of these calculations, he started to notice a pattern. The farms all owed a fraction of their value. The problem was simply that the fraction they owed they weren't going to be able to pay so long as things stayed the way they were. But it could be, Lucius thought, that selling of a portion of their assets: machines or land, might be enough for the bank to hold off on foreclosure for a year or two. Then, like Veronica Hallstaff, they'd have to pray for rain or buy seeds from Snzl.

He ran this approach by Oliver. He was only concerned with money coming in to the bank. If money was coming in, he didn't care what needed to happen, "You might still have an uphill climb. It's hard to convince these folks to stay and part with some of their land. Especially if it means a subdivision is moving in where their soybeans used to grow."

Oliver thought about this. He made some calls. Some local agricultural clubs were interested in land they could use to demonstrate techniques to high school students. The university was interested in land for purposes of agricultural testing. And a land developer told him anything that came open would be considered for a housing development. All that remained was to actually convince a farmer this was a good idea.

Cornstalks stood late into the fall curved somberly by the wind. They spoke of a certain defiance of the elements, and a certain neglect by the Wilkerson farm. Mr. Wilkerson had done the math on the cost of harvesting his corn this year, and it was greater than the return would be if he sold it. That's how bad the yield was: not worth the cost to harvest.

It also looked like the bank would be foreclosing on the farm anyway, so why prepare the ground for future seasons? The corn was doomed to stand against the winter, signaling poverty and decay to everyone approaching Hardy from the West.

Lucius Stancroft drove by the Wilkerson farm, his black Cadillac against the wilted corn made the scene gloomier. He was driving slow because he was nervous about the errand he was on. His entire approach depended on other folks agreeing with him. He would have to be a salesman to pull this off.

Whatever the future held, creeping along in his car didn't make the scene any cheerier.

He turned in at the Applegate farm, and pulled slowly up the gravel driveway. Harvey Applegate was again waiting for him on the porch. This time Lucius was dressed in a business suit, navy blue, with a three button jacket. He got out of the car and checked his buttons from top to bottom, "Always, sometimes, never" he muttered to himself. Then he straightened his shoulders and faced the man on the porch.

"Your uncle send you out here to do his dirty work for him?"

"Yes he did," Lucius said.

"Why? Is he too big a coward to face me man to man?"

"No he isn't. He prefers to send me on these now."

"Why?"

"Because I'm a mean sumbitch and nobody wants any trouble."

Both men laughed.

Lucius pulled out a map and began, "You don't have to foreclose. You can sell this hilly field here," he pointed at the map, "bad for growing, a pain for you to deal with, but just fine for building a housing development. That's not what you'd rather do, I understand. But it would save your farm, at least for a year or two til we get better weather."

"Well..."

"Of course you could always keep it and develop it yourself."

"No, I'll be farming. Who has time for that?"

"Who has time for that," Lucius echoed.

"What a relief!" Harvey beamed, "I was sure I was sunk. Some days of course I'd be glad to be done with it. But then I don't know what else I'd do. Thank you for helping me save my farm. Most of it anyway."

"It's the neighborly thing to do," Lucius smiled.

The Turkelson Murders

The year before they caught James Francis Turkelson, all we knew was that some terminally ill people had died earlier than their physicians had predicted. No one would have guessed there was a connection between him and the deaths, which seems odd in hindsight. Maybe that's why so many people now claim they knew it all along.

It was August and we were grateful to be back in school, away from the long monotony of not having enough money to have fun.

I was sixteen years old that fall. The trees around Hardy were browning early due to the drought, and Lake Jefferson was down.

Ana Thompson was my girlfriend then. Hardy seemed like a big world to her the previous year, after having been homeschooled until she was fourteen. When she first came to school, I was officially designated by the school administrators to be the one to show her around. Then I became a person she trusted. Then I became a close friend. And then we ended up being a little more than friends. All because we were stuck together by unseen bureaucratic forces.

We were walking around the lake after school, holding hands, talking about the future abstractly, the way one talks about boron or silicon. I felt like it was my duty to explain everything to her, which must have seemed extraordinarily patronizing and irksome to her. Nevertheless, there I was, explaining to her that Indiana University in Bloomington was much bigger than the Hardy Community College up the street, when coming the opposite way around the path was Hortense Pemberton.

Hortense Pemberton, née Smith, was born in Oklahoma during the Dust Bowl. She married Thomas Pemberton of the Hardy, Indiana Pembertons in 1961 at the age of twenty-nine. This marriage was a considerable improvement on her financial and social position at the time. She'd come from poverty, and now married into the family that owned a bank and a local paper.

She had been told throughout her marriage, or for as much of it as her mother-in-law had been alive, that she simply wasn't Pemberton material.

"My Thomas could have found any woman in the world to marry, and he used that power to marry a poor Okie," she'd said once, "A Smith, as well. What a pedigree! 'What did your ancestors do?' they'll ask your children. What can they say? 'They bent over a forge making horseshoes'?"

Hortense did not stand for this kind of talk one bit, "Now you listen to me, the Dust Bowl killed both of my sisters and all three of my brothers."

"Oh, lovely! That sweetens the pot, does it?"

"It killed all five of them, but not me. I was born tough, and I aim to die tough. In between I mean to be even tougher. If you think some jabbering about how high in the air your nose will go is going to run me off, Mrs. Pemberton," her mother-in-law refusing Hortense the privilege of using her first name, "you have another think coming."

This kind of talk made Thomas proud. He hadn't set out to find a woman his mother would disapprove of, exactly. He'd set out to find a woman he loved, and Miss Hortense Smith was so refreshingly strong, so novel, so other, that he couldn't help falling for her.

They married in the early sixties, late in life for a woman to get married, his mother had thought. Jefferson was born two years later. Then Thomas went to serve in Vietnam and never returned.

Hortense's mother-in-law passed away after that, which left the lot of the family money and businesses to Hortense and her son.

She ran it all herself with tenacity and vigor. The family wealth expanded, and the business grew. In Hardy, she was so revered she became like a god in whose presence one dared not speak.

As such, I averted my eyes as she approached us at the lake.

"Whole damn town's full of people too scared to talk to me," she muttered.

"How are you today, Mrs. Pemberton?" asked Ana. I snapped to attention as the words came out of her mouth, mentally preparing for the inexorable lecture about common folk like us not accosting our betters with useless words.

"Do you really want to know?" she asked. I braced myself further.

"Yes, of course," said Ana, "You seemed like you were miles away just now. Is something the matter?"

"Something is always the matter, dear. But you can only do so much in a lifetime."

"I see," Ana said.

"Ah, you see!" laughed Mrs. Pemberton, "Well chance'd be a fine thing."

"I'm sorry?"

Mrs. Pemberton looked us over for a second, "Never you mind about that. Just try not to step in any of the dog shit up the trail, okay?"

Ana said "Okay," but Mrs. Pemberton had already walked past shaking her head.

After she had gotten out of earshot, Ana said, "She always seems so sad."

"Sad?!" I said, surprised, "she's the richest old lady in town!"

"So?"

"So how can she be sad?" I asked.

"What's stopping her?" she stumped me with that one.

There, fishing from the dock, we saw James Francis Turkelson. He waved at us. We waved at him.

James Francis Turkelson, called "Tom" around town, as in "Tom Turkey," a play on his surname, was born in Hardy in 1968. He was, reputedly, a fantastic chess player. Later on in life, he organized the federal penitentiary in Terre Haute's first ever chess league, so much did he love the game.

I knew him as a local fixture. He spent a lot of time outdoors fishing, hunting, or playing tennis. He was present at every home basketball game at the high school, and even applied numerous times to coach the baseball team. He knew all the statistics for a lot of the high school sports teams in Southern Indiana. That was something I assumed adult males just acquired over time. They'd breathe it in from Indiana's atmosphere and incorporate it into their being.

My father seemed to like him in an at-arm's-length kind of way. My mother, on the other hand, adored him. She saw in his constant presence at the school's sporting events a model for community involvement that we should all aspire to.

She went so far as to hang a number of attributes on him he had no title to. In my mother's words he was "a model citizen, charitable, funny, and connected to the things that really matter in a small town." Looking back, I think my mother may have had a bit of a crush on the man.

His victims were all his patients on Hospice care.

A few weeks after the walk at the lake, Ana ran into Hortense Pemberton at the grocery store.

"Hello, Mrs. Pemberton," she said.

Hortense looked at her very carefully. "Have we met?" she said.

"Not properly. We saw one another at the lake a few weeks ago. I was walking with my boyfriend."

"Ah yes. I told you not to step in the shit."

"That's right," Ana said.

"Well did you?"

"Did I what?"

"Step in any?"

"No," Ana said, confused and embarrassed.

"Good. Glad I could help," Hortense said and started walking away.

"I'd like to help you!" Ana called after her.

"Help me?" she said turning around, "Do you know who I am?"

"The richest lady in town. I don't care. I'd like to help you."

"It's good that you don't care but—" she stopped talking. Her eyes focused on something behind Ana, and she lost interest in everything else.

"But...?" Ana looked behind her. James Francis Turkelson was in the store shopping. He was reading the labels on cans of beans.

"See that man? I don't trust him," Hortense said.

"Oh really? Why?"

"It's just a feeling I have. I don't know. I can't explain it, but I don't trust him."

"I could follow him around and see what he's up to. Would that help you?"

Hortense thought that over for a second, shrugged and said "Sure kid, knock yourself out."

Ana brought this plan to me later that evening. We'd arranged to meet and go for a walk.

"We should follow this Turkelson fellow around," she said.

"What? Why are we doing that?"

"I ran into Mrs. Pemberton at the store today. She said it would help her."

"Help her? How?"

"She doesn't trust him."

"Huh? Why not? He's just an ordinary guy!" I protested.

"I don't trust him either," she said.

"Have you ever spoken with him?"

"Well, no..."

"Okay. Just curious."

"You said he was always at the basketball games, isn't that weird?"

"This is Indiana. High school basketball is life here."

"So you don't think that's weird?"

"Not even a little bit."

"How could we prove he's not up to something sketchy?" she changed tactics.

I only needed a second to ponder this to see I'd been cornered. "I guess we should follow him around and clear his name," I said.

"Thank you!" she said.

It suddenly became hard to find JFT. We had expected to just go on a walk and see him. It seemed like we saw him a lot more often under normal circumstances than we really did. And now that we were trying to find him, we were realizing the town was a little bigger than we thought, and the chances of being guaranteed to see a particular person were a little worse than we thought.

"We're going to have to keep trying," Ana said after a week of dead ends. I was fine with this. It meant spending more time with my girlfriend. Although the time we were spending together didn't strike me as particularly romantic: walking to the lake, walking to the grocery store, peeking in restaurants, all trying to catch of a glimpse of a man who, might or might not be up to something shady.

I'm sure I was less than charming during this period. It's probable I was even a little—and I hate to admit it—whiny.

One Tuesday I asked if we could just stay in for a night. Ana said, "It might be the night we find him. What if we miss that chance just staying at home?"

We didn't see him that night.

A week and change later, on a Thursday, I got my dad's permission to borrow the car for the night. I asked Ana if she wanted to go to the drive in outside Valico. Ana said, "This is a great opportunity to cover more ground! We won't have to walk everywhere! We're sure to find him tonight."

Still no sign of James Francis Turkelson.

About three weeks or so past the only time my dad lent me the car that summer, we finally had a sighting. Ana and I were at the lake walking, and there he was, fishing off the bank again. He was engrossed in something going wrong with his rod. He didn't see us.

We carefully moved up the bank and found a spot where we felt safely out of sight, but we were able to see him struggling with his line.

After struggling a few more minutes, Tom Turkey gave up on fishing, packed up, and headed home.

We followed him home, keeping a safe distance where we felt sure he wouldn't notice he was being followed.

I was terrified the entire walk. There was nothing to fear from this walk. If he had noticed we were following him, it's unlikely he would have thought anything of it. There were a hundred innocent reasons for someone to be walking the same way he was. But we knew what we were up to, and we projected that knowledge onto everyone else. We feared every glance. We suspected every movement.

Luckily we learned that night where he lived: information that in hindsight we probably could have retrieved from a phone book. He lived very close to the lake.

There was nothing nefarious in his walking home with his pole and tackle box, so Ana and I went home with a new starting point for all subsequent ventures.

The next morning we met outside James Francis Turkelson's house, with a plan to follow him around all day. He was a Hospice nurse, and that day he walked over to Maple Street to an older ranch-style.

He went from house to house all day, and from the outside, nothing changed all day except the angle of the sun.

Ana and I struggled to appear inconspicuous. It was hard to stand outside residential addresses all day without raising an eyebrow or two.

"Are you sure it's such a good idea to stay out on the street all day?" I asked.

"Well, what if he leaves? What if he goes somewhere and does something, I don't know...suspicious?"

"What if he doesn't, though? What if he comes out of there at the end of the day and just goes home and we've spent a whole day just standing here trying not to get noticed by anybody?"

"I just have a feeling we're going to miss something," Ana said.

"I mean right now we're missing our lives. They're not happening because we're doing this."

"You mean you wouldn't be spending time with your girlfriend?"

"I mean me and my girlfriend would be doing something fun!"

"So hanging out with your girlfriend isn't fun?"

"That's not what I meant."

"It's what you said."

"I just mean we could be having more fun...together...than we're having now. We're just standing. We're not even watching something happen. Nothing is happening."

"Well, maybe we can have a nice conversation."

"Okay. What do you want to talk about?"

"I don't know."

"Hmm. Me either," I said.

We sank back into the glum, uninterrupted boredom of staring at the outside of hospice patients' houses.

At the end of the workday, James Francis Turkelson walked home. We hid behind a garden shed to avoid being seen by him as he passed by. We followed him home, staying out of his sight. Not that he ever looked over his shoulder. A fact I mentioned: "If he were really up to something wouldn't he act more nervous? Be looking over his shoulder? Something?"

"What if he has no conscience?" Ana asked. She had an answer for all of my objections.

When we got back to his house, we decided to call it a day and go home. Frankly I was a little relieved to get a break from her. We agreed—and I'm stretching the truth a bit by saying "we"—to meet back there the next morning and start a new day of vigilance.

The next day began in much the same way. We met at
James Francis Turkelson's house and followed him around from
house to house.

I was particularly complain-y that day. It was a gorgeous
day for golfing or hiking or a picnic or anything but following a
hospice nurse from house to house. I said so,

"What if we take one day off from this? We could do
anything. Anything we wanted. Just don't make me do this
another day."

"Make you? I'm not making you do this. You can go if you
don't want to spend time with me."

It was a masterpiece of a thing to say, I thought. She had
me caught in her web. But just like a fly, I couldn't help
squirming.

"I do want to spend time with you, just doing something
else."

"Well this is what I'm doing today. Take it or leave it."

I groaned and stayed put.

We nearly completed the same circuit as the day before.
At the next to last house, Ana sighed.

"Getting bored?" I asked hopefully.

"Frustrated," she said, "If only we could get closer, we
could see what he's up to in there."

"Up to? He's a nurse. He's taking care of people."

"What if he's stealing from them or, I don't know.
Something shady."

"I don't know, I think he's probably not."

"You just don't want to believe he's up to something. Let's
get closer and find out."

Now I started to panic. It's one thing to stand up the street from a house and not be seen by someone inside, but start pressing your face against their windows and they just might notice.

"I don't think that's a good idea," I said, "We're safer over here."

"Safer but we can't see anything. We're wasting our time standing all the way over here. What are we even doing?"

"That's kind of what I've been saying..."

"So you want to go closer then?"

"No. I want to go home."

"Go home then," she said. She said it seriously and I took it seriously.

I walked to the end of the street and looked back. She was sneaking up to the picture window looking out at the street. I figured she'd get caught doing that. For a split second I thought the chivalrous thing to do might be to swoop in and save her from whatever the consequences might be. The fear of facing those consequences myself caught up to me and spurred me on home.

I walked home and wondered what all of this meant for me and Ana. I assumed she'd get in trouble for peeking into strangers' houses, see the error of her ways, and come back to me and apologize.

"No big deal," I'd say, "I have no hard feelings." Then we could borrow my dad's car and go to a drive-in or something romantic.

About twenty minutes after I left, I heard police sirens. I followed the sound and tried to track where they were heading. I knew already. They were coming from where we'd just been. The consequences I'd feared were more serious than I ever could have realized. Somebody must have called the law on Ana.

Once again the old sense of patronizing chivalry spoke up saying I should rush in and save her. Surely it's too late if the police are there, I thought. She must be running. If so, she'll come to my house. So it's best to stay home and be prepared to hide her from the law.

So I went home and waited all evening. No Ana.

My dad came home that evening and asked to see me. That sealed it. I was in for it. No more drive-ins.

"Were you with that girl Ana Thompson this afternoon?" he asked me.

"I was for a while and then I came home," I sighed.

"So you missed all the action?" he asked.

"I...umm...what action?" I stammered.

"She caught that murderer!" he said, glowing with pride.

"Huh?" was all I could manage. I was simultaneously relieved and disappointed: Ana wasn't in any trouble, but that meant she wasn't coming back to hide out with me.

My mom had come into the room to hear what the fuss was about. "Oh I'm sure your father was exaggerating, dear."

"Not exaggerating, no! She had a suspicion something was going on in this house. So she peeked in the window and there was that James Francis Turkelson," he said.

It dawned on me now what I must have looked like to Ana. I flatly refused to go look in that window out of fear, and now she's a local hero.

"Someone killed him?" my mom gasped.

"No," my dad said, "he was smothering Mrs. Windermere to death with a pillow."

"James was? James *Turkelson*?" my mom said. She needed to sit down.

"He was!" Dad really enjoyed rubbing it in, "So Ana ran off to call the police and they caught him still in the house! They put Ana's testimony in front of him and he confessed to the whole thing. Apparently he's killed seventeen people this way!"

My mom looked ghostly white. She just sat on the couch muttering "Oh my. Oh my. Oh my."

"And our son's girlfriend caught the serial killer," my dad said.

It suddenly became very hard for me to get in contact with Ana on the phone, in person, or however else. I would call her house and her mom would just tell me she couldn't come to the phone at the moment. I was too young to read between the lines, and I just keep leaving messages with her mom. This went on for weeks before my dad pulled me aside and said, "Her mom has the messages you've left. You don't need to leave any more of them."

It didn't register with me that she was simply not going to allow me to weigh her down anymore until I saw her from across the street as she was walking into a side door at the Clapford Gazette—the paper Hortense Pemberton owned.

I ran to the door to follow her in, but there was a sign that said employees only, and you needed a passcode to unlock the door. I stood there on the sidewalk, not knowing how to open the door.

The Man from Indianapolis

Jake pulled the van into a pole barn in a clearing in the woods outside of Valico. He parked the van, shut off the engine, got out and closed the door to the barn.

A man who called himself "Gator" was there. Gator was a nervous man. He was constantly in fear of being caught or being followed.

Jake met up with Gator once a month to sell electronics he'd found when breaking into people's houses. He'd offload them into Gator's trailer, and off he'd go. Gator worked for someone up in Indianapolis who sold those electronics on to other folks. Gator called the guy he worked for "Mr. Smith" and routinely made a point of mentioning that wasn't his real name.

Jake didn't care much about what all happened after they met, so long as he got paid.

Gator was especially nervous tonight, "Man you hear about that bombing over in Crothersville?" Gator asked.

"The what?"

"Some fella who sells to Mr. Smith, man. His whole place got blown up."

"On accident?"

Gator just looked and blinked at Jake for a second, "Are you stupid?"

"Well..."

"Of course it wasn't no damn accident. Something's going down. I don't know what. I haven't heard anything. And I'm not stupid enough to ask and end up being the next guy you hear a story about."

"Right," Jake said. It was a default of his when he had no idea what someone was talking about it. It made him seem both knowledgeable and positive. He liked that.

"All right man, it's twenty-five hundred."

"Hold up. What? It's five thousand."

"Nah man, times are tight and that means we got to be tight. That means your belt has got to be tight. Twenty-five hundred."

Jake took a deep breath. He wasn't accustomed to anyone trying to push him around. He felt like the one generally doing the pushing around in life.

"No deal, man."

"No...no deal?" Gator couldn't believe what he was hearing.

"No."

"Dude, do you know who I work for?"

"I don't. Let me talk to him," Jake was proud of the effect he was having on Gator.

"You do not want this."

"I need more than twenty five hundred though."

Gator changed suddenly. Jake was not having the effect he thought he was, "Okay...Here's what happens in this situation you stupid dude-bro: you take the money Mr. Smith sent for you, or someone comes down here and pulls your guts out through your ears. That's whether or not the police find you carrying all these stolen goods. And hey, someone might just tip them off."

"Is that supposed to scare me?"

"Dude... fine."

"You're giving me my five grand?"

"No, I'm sending you out to find out what happens next."

"Oooh, spooky," Jake laughed.

Gator shook his head sadly and opened the door to the barn.

Jake chuckled to himself. He started the van and began rolling out slowly. *These theatrics*, he thought to himself, *They can't not take the stuff, they need it too much. Any second he'll stop me and give in.*

Gator did not stop him. He'd gone into a room in the corner of the barn and shut the door behind him.

Jake took the van as gingerly as he could down unlit backroads to a farm owned by a business associate of his named Terry. All the way imagining he was about to see headlights come over the hill, or that he was hearing another motor out there in the inky dark. He made it to Terry's without incident.

Terry was a sort of sponsor for Jake: he got him information, he hid the van. In exchange, he took some profit.

Terry was, as usual, waiting in the barn when Jake pulled in, ready to collect his money.

"They wouldn't pay," Jake said as he got out of the van.

"Wouldn't pay?" Terry echoed, "What do you mean they wouldn't pay?"

"They cut the price in half and I said no deal."

"Oh I see, so when you said they wouldn't pay, what you meant was they would pay, but you wouldn't sell."

"Look Terry, they'll come around. They need this stuff."

"Uh huh, and we need to get rid of it. I'd a thousand times rather take half the money than sit around here holding stolen goods. They've got us over a barrel, dummy."

"It was my call, so I made it."

"Real great. You have none of the risk, dude! The stuff is here on my property! If they find it here, I go down, not you. Unless I say your name."

"They're not going to find the stuff. Chill."

"You don't know what these people will do. They don't even have to get their hands dirty, they can just leave an anonymous tip with the police and that's it. We're done. I'm done anyway."

Jake thought about this and remembered something, "Did you hear about a bombing in Crothersville?"

"What? No. This may come as a shock to you, but I don't keep track of what's going on in every tiny town in Indiana."

"Dude, it was a guy that works for Mr. Smith."

"Who?"

"The guy Gator works for."

Terry's face turned red, "What?! Did he tell you about this before or after you turned down his money?"

"Uhh, before?"

"God you're stupid!"

"No, I..."

"Some guy is gonna come down here and burn my farm down because you got stupid," Terry said.

"Nobody's going to burn anything down."

"Dude...Indy isn't that far away. He's probably already on his way, and he'll be here in ninety minutes."

"No everything is cool."

"Is it cool?"

"I think so," Jake shrugged.

"You *think* so?"

"Yeah they're gonna call us up and give us our money and we'll all be square."

"Why in the flat-ironed hell are they going to do that when they can just dispose of us and move on?"

"They need the stuff," Jake said.

"Are you listening? They don't need us. We need them! All they need is no headache. You just gave them a headache, so now they're going to have to take care of it."

"I don't know man..."

"Listen, tomorrow morning you go see my uncle Rick in Steamsburg. He used to deal with these people. He's not much now, but maybe he can get us out of this with our lives."

Jake drove to Rick's house in Steamsburg in the morning. When he arrived, Rick was standing in his garage with the door open. He had his back turned to the door, hunched over a piece of wood he was hacking away at with a chisel.

"I assume you're Jake," he said.

Jake stopped in his tracks, "How....how did you know?"

Rick stopped working and turned around, "Oh! Ha! Ha! It worked. I've been saying that every two minutes all morning..." he laughed.

"So, you knew I was coming?" Jake asked.

"Yeah dummy," Rick said, "Terry wasn't sending you to your death. If you ever want to send someone to their death, tell them to come here, and don't tell me they're coming."

"Oh that's great! I might have a guy after me I can just send him your way! Terry said you could help."

"Yeah, I heard about this," Rick said, massaging the tip of his chisel methodically, "You can't send them here."

"I thought you just said..."

"Yeah I know what I said. But listen, you might be a gunslinger taking on Jesse James. That's one thing. But if a fella shows up with a Sherman tank, it doesn't matter how quick your trigger finger is."

"What?" Jake was confused.

"This fella after you, he's a lot bigger fish than you or me."

"So you know who it is."

"I know who it is."

"How can I avoid him?"

"I wouldn't if I were you," Rick said.

"What?"

"You go to him. You show him your face. You show him respect. You tell him you made a mistake. And you most definitely take whatever they're offering."

"This guy's coming to kill me though," Jake said.

"Ehhh, he might. He's here to eliminate a threat. Show him you're not a threat. You start hiding from him, he's going to think you're running to the police, and then they have a problem. When they think they have a problem, they deal with it. So, you dumb punk, show him you're not a problem."

The man from Indianapolis moved through Valico like a shadow. People who saw him weren't sure they had, and when they did a double-take he wasn't still there. Most thought they'd imagined it. He wore a bright red suit and tie. It caught the eye, but he tended not to linger in one place to give folks a second look.

There was one man who saw him from, as it were, the wrong angle, and to him the man in the red suit's trick was as transparent as seeing a magician's act from behind. The man who saw him was a retiree named Ogbert Fraser. Oggie was a curious personable fellow who'd been in car sales until he felt he didn't need to be anymore, and then moved on to a new phase of his life where he was determined to fritter away time gossiping with other old men, chatting with visitors at Zeb's Diner, fishing off the dock at Lake Jefferson, and so forth. He made it a goal to never have an agenda for the day, so he could follow wherever the wind blew.

And today the wind was blowing toward a curious seedy little fellow in a red suit who was trying not to be seen for some reason. Oggie thought he might advise the man not to wear red if he wanted to evade detection.

He looked again and the man was gone.

"What'll you get into today?" the server at the diner asked him.

"Looks like I have a little mystery to unravel," he said trying to appear as perplexing as the little man.

The man in the red suit nosed out the location of Gator's farm and made his way there deliberately and quietly.

He walked into the barn door at Gator's place and stopped.

"Where are you, you delightful local creature?" he said into the emptiness.

He heard nothing in reply save some footsteps in the office. He walked in their direction.

Gator did not hear or notice him come in. He'd decided to be prepared to leave if things went sideways, so he was busy packing up essentials into a gym bag in case he needed them.

The man walked into his office and shut the door behind him. Gator looked up and froze.

"There you are, black sheep!" the man said, "Where is your wool?"

"Do...do you work for Mr. Smith?"

The man ignored the question, "In a profession such as yours and such as mine, we often find dishonest creatures, don't we?" the man asked.

"Excuse me?"

"Such is the Life," he said, "Folks want to get by and get ahead. Some of those folks will do it by any means necessary. Wouldn't you know it, some of those means are unsavory, cruel and dishonest."

"Umm, sure?"

"Part of the path in this life is trying to work out who it is that's being honest, and who it is you're going to have a problem with. Problems...why you have to deal with problems. Otherwise, they become bigger problems, and bigger still after that. We can't have that can we?"

"No sir. That's very well spoken. I-"

"Now...right now...I need to know. Are you an honest creature, or do we have a problem?"

"I'm honest, sir."

"Is that a fact?"

"Yes."

"I understand there is a problem around here though. Maybe it's you, maybe it's not. Either way, I've been asked to...research...this problem."

"This fella Jake. He come in here last night same as regular. I told him the price was cut. I could only offer him half what he was used to getting. Now that came straight from the man, Mr. Smith: prices are half now. Did that make things rough for us little guys? Yes. But I stick to it, sir. I'm honest. I'm not a problem like you said."

"So Jake, he's a problem?"

"He thought I'd have to give in and pay the normal amount, so he drove off without anything changing hands."

"I see. And now he's...evading the police, I assume?"

"Not sure. I guess. I called them and said I'd seen a suspicious van driving around."

"You called the police?" the man asked.

"Yeah I figured they could deal with him, and we wouldn't have to."

"Sir, you're too honest," the man said, taking a knife out from the pocket of his suit jacket.

Jake stopped to eat on his way back from Steamsburg, and then made his way carefully over to Terry's place. He tried to ensure he wasn't being followed and wasn't taking the obvious path. He was proud of his craftiness. So much had happened that called into question his savvy, his ability to be tactical and think strategically. Even the smallest win in this department was something to celebrate.

So he was pleased with himself until he pulled out of the final turn to Terry's place and saw seven squad cars in his driveway making a real show of having their red and blue lights on.

Gator said he'd call the police, Jake thought. It was exactly what Terry was worried about, and now here it was, an ambush. An innocent bystander getting hurt in all of this.

No, he reminded himself, not exactly innocent. He was knowingly harboring stolen goods after all.

Jake drove on past the farm, feeling that putting his car in reverse would probably draw some unwanted attention from the police officers.

He went to visit Gator to see if he could help him find whoever it was that was out there looking for him. He felt it best to take whatever money they were offering, not to cause a ruckus, and not mention the squadron he'd just seen at Terry's homestead. "Terry who?" he thought.

Jake pulled into Gator's garage. The man in the red suit was leaning against the wall with his arms folded.

"Are you...?"

"I most assuredly am, you little cupcake."

"What?"

"Are you a dishonest creature?"

"Umm, no," Jake said quietly.

"Ah, well I know that you are, Jacob."

"It's Jake."

"Surely your parents named you Jacob," the man said.

"Nope. It's Jake."

"That's disgusting," the man said.

"It is what it is."

"Even more disgusting," he said to himself, "Do we have a problem, Jacob?"

"No sir, we do not. I'm perfectly happy with twenty-five hundred."

"Twenty-five? No sir. Five hundred."

"Five hundred? Man I have to pay rent!"

"That's adorable!"

"What?"

"Lots of people have to pay rent, Jacob. I am not expected to care about any of them, am I?"

"But this is how I make my money, man."

"Ah, well, I suppose you think you're being treated unfairly, hmm? Perhaps you can call the authorities and complain?"

Jake looked off into space and sighed, "Five hundred is fine."

"Excellent. Now, where are the items in question?"

Jake froze, "Well," he gulped.

"Uh-huh..." the man said, trying to coax out an answer.

"They're in a van."

"Excellent, and where might one find this...van?"

"It's at my friend Terry's house."

"Well let's go and get it. I'll ride with you."

"We can't, umm, we can't do that."

"Jacob, you told me you weren't a problem."

"I'm not."

"Then what's the problem?"

"A load of cops. A battalion of cops. I just drove by there and they were everywhere."

"Police?"

"Yeah, Gator said he was going to call the cops."

"Gator?"

"Yeah, where is he? This is his barn. I came to ask him where I could find you but you were here, so I forgot about him. Where is he?"

"Never mind that. You're telling me, the van full of stolen goods, the van for which you just negotiated a price with me, is in the middle of a platoon of police officers who've been tipped off about a van carrying stolen goods?"

"They..." Jake was stunned, but thought about the situation and realized that was the only thing they could have been tipped off about, "Yes. Yes it is."

The man sighed, and reached into his jacket pocket, "You're too honest as well," he said as he pulled a out a knife.

Just then a Louisville Slugger came down on the man's head. He crumpled to the ground.

Jake stared at the empty space in front of him trying to make sense of what just happened.

"Damn good shot," Oggie Fraser said.

"What?" Jake looked around bewildered. He finally saw an old man standing right in front of him. He had no idea where he came from or how long he'd been there.

"I knew, all day I knew. I saw this fella in town this morning and I just knew it was bad news. Then here he is pulling a knife on you."

"Who...who are you?"

"Ogbert. Folks call me Oggie."

"I mean, who are you...to this situation? Why are you here?"

"Like I said, I saw this fella. I knew he was bad news, so I tracked him. I couldn't save your friend back there, but at least I could save you."

"My...friend...?"

"It's best you don't look. Police are coming. They'll take care of him, take care of you. Hell, they will probably take care of me."

"You don't understand. *This* dude is bad, but he works for someone worse. And they think I'm a problem. I have to tell them I'm not a problem."

"Well you are now, like it or not. But you just talk with the police about it. Maybe they can get you in one of those witness protection deals. They can't put you in a worse place than Clapford County, Indiana," Oggie roared with laughter.

Jake thought about this as he helped Oggie tie up the man in the red suit while they waited for the police.

Oggie just imagined how pleased everyone would be to hear a new story back at Zeb's Diner.

The Last Show

J Kamer got off the bus in Newark, Ohio. He held his guitar case out in front of him so as not to bang the case against the handrails. His suitcase he let drag behind with an impressive and carefree clatter. He looked up and down the road. Nobody was at the station to meet him. That was normal. He'd done hundreds of these and only been met at the bus station a handful of times. Funny how making a point of telling show organizers that you were arriving by bus and didn't have a car made almost no impact on them.

There was a sort of bar-slash-theatre place called The Marshes he was booked at that evening. He just had to walk there. It wasn't a big town. It wasn't a big deal.

There was a romanticized notion in his head of a man with a guitar hanging over his shoulder, walking along a dusty highway. In spite of the ground being verdant and lush in Ohio much like it was in Valico, and in spite of the cumbersome weary suitcase dragging along behind him, he felt like it must be a pretty awesome sight: a picture of a true bohemian pursuing his dream.

He always felt like he looked picturesque.

The Marshes was about a mile away, and he lumbered over there with his cases. At sixty he moved slower than he realized. He was always surprised at how long it took him to walk places. It didn't matter, he had ample time to get there. He had hours to kill before the show. It was some kind of showcase with two other singer songwriters. There was Lorna Williams from Cleveland. He knew her by reputation. She was one of the new kids who sounded and wrote like they'd been around a hundred years. He hated it, but he respected it. Dylan was one of those at one time. *Fair is fair*, he thought, *if I am gonna let Dylan slide, I guess I can make space for Lorna Williams.*

Also on the bill was Dan "Hammer" Jones, who J knew for years and years now. He was a sad thing to see live. Nobody had the heart to tell him it wasn't going to happen for him. This showcase was Hammer's big show for the year. He wasn't ever going to break through if he hadn't done it by now.

Even so, and even after performing thirty-five years and never making it, there was an earnestness and a sincerity to Hammer Jones.

J Kamer arrived at The Marshes and said hello to the show runner—a vacant sort of fellow named Jack. In a colorless monotone Jack said, "I'm glad you could be here."

"Couldn't be happier to be here," J answered lie for lie.

"Lorna's here in the show room," Jack said.

"Thank you," J said and took his leave.

The Marshes was laid out like a lot of venues J'd been in. A bar in the room in the front, and a larger room in the back with a stage. This place at least had theater seating. It was the home stage of a theater troupe as well as an improv group. Both acting and comedy made J feel inadequate and illegitimate. *Serious things happen here. It's nice of them to let us play,* he thought.

Lorna Williams was on the stage arranging what equipment there was to arrange. With three singer songwriters playing unaccompanied, it was just checking a single microphone and making sure the guitar didn't drown out the vocals.

"Hammer Jones?" she asked.

"J Kamer," he said, setting his guitar case down on the stage.

"Oh dude," she said, "It's nice to meet you. I have your album *The Girl and The Bear*. It's so personal and strong. I loved it."

"Oh thank you. It's nice to meet you too."

A beat lingered in the air, and J felt the inequality of having his record praised but not being able to return the compliment for Lorna. He knew what she sounded like because she had such a strong social media "presence." It was something J had never bothered to spend time on and now the world had passed him by. Albums, he didn't know if she had any, songs though. He could say something about a song, "I was just trying to remember the name of this song of yours and I'm sorry I can't. It's about a woman who drops her husband's body into a ravine where it won't ever be found."

"Song is called 'Mother's Day.'"

"Man alive, there's so much in that one. Reminds me of Dylan when he was young, and he already wrote like he'd lived it all and knew it all."

"Oh, umm, thank you for that. I've never been a big Dylan fan though."

He looked at her for a moment, "To each his own, I guess."

"Do you know Hammer?" she asked.

"Oh sure, I bet we've done twenty shows like this over the years."

"Really?"

"Yeah well, he's from Louisville and I'm from Valico, Indiana. So we're not too far away from one another."

"Cool. I've never been to Valico in Indiana, but I've been to Churubusco."

"I don't know it. Where is it?"

"Close to Fort Wayne, I think."

"Ahh," J said. Half of Kentucky was closer than Fort Wayne.

Behind J at the door there was a commotion of someone entering the room, "J Kamer! How are ya man?" J and Lorna looked up at Hammer Jones. The three of them greeted one another.

Hammer wore a canvas proletariat hat with leather bill, a blue brown wool blazer with a white button down shirt beneath, and tan corduroy pants. The ensemble was carefully engineered to give one the impression that before you stood a serious revolutionary figure. You were to ignore the cozy bourgeois reality of the man wearing the costume.

Hammer was a gifted telecommunications consultant who had a downtown office with a view of Louisville and the Ohio River. He worked for the multinational conglomerate Macrotech, and was compensated handsomely. J had always thought Hammer could honestly have been a great songwriter if only he'd needed to be. As it was, he was living very comfortably from solving people's communications problems. If he'd had to write good songs and be an engaging performer in order to eat, it might have gotten more of his effort over the years. Instead it was a hobby, and a hobby he expected sooner or later someone was just going to come along and pay him for.

"It's an honor to play with you both," Lorna said, "I am hoping after tonight we can arrange to do a few more of these."

"That'd be great!" Hammer said, hoping to ride the coattails of a rising star.

"I might as well tell you both, I guess," J said, "but this is my last show."

"Wait," said Hammer, "you don't mean you're quitting."

"Yeah. I'm done. Someone asked me to do a show tomorrow and I told them to go suck a radish. I'm through."

"I'm curious, why are you quitting?" Lorna asked.

"I'm ridiculous!" he said, "Look at me: I'm an old man with all my best days behind me, riding a bus from town to town, playing in front of folks that stopped caring a long time ago. They used to see something in me. Potential, I guess. I let them down, and they gave up on me. I couldn't win them back now if I wanted to."

Hammer looked hurt and betrayed. He couldn't bring himself to speak.

"I mean, your record is brilliant," Lorna said.

"You know what else it is? Fifteen years old. With no follow-up. None coming either. The well's dry. Maybe if I quit and the inspiration starts coming back I'll do something. But it would have to be something powerful to get me on the road again."

"You're ridiculous?" Hammer finally spoke, "You? There's not a ridiculous bone in your body. You're a great singer and a great songwriter. I mean, dammit J, if you're ridiculous, what do you think of me?"

There was an awkward truthful answer to that question, but J didn't want to say it out loud. He'd already struck a nerve by announcing his retirement. It didn't seem right to compound the issue by stating the facts as he saw them about Hammer. He opened his mouth, but nothing came out. If anyone asked, he thought he could say he tried to be honest.

"Well?" Hammer persisted.

"I don't think this is a fair line of inquiry," Lorna said, "Let's celebrate your career. I'm featuring at the very end of it, a footnote to your history. It's an honor."

"Uh, thank you," J said.

"Yeah, a real honor," Hammer said moodily. He went to the back of the stage and began fiddling around with his guitar. He tuned it, and once he was done he tuned it again. After that, he tuned it once more for good measure.

J sat in the front row of the seats and took time to observe it all. Everyone has their own way of preparing for a performance. A lot of people like to go find somewhere quiet they can be alone to plan or warm up. Some people pretend like nothing is happening, and then walk on stage when their name is called as if they were just finding out they were on the bill that night. J had always gone to the back somewhere and agonized over song order. For the past sixth months he'd played exactly the same forty-minute set every time out. The same songs, in the same order, in the same way. This look a lot of the planning out of it, and now before shows started he had a lot more time to look around and get in other people's way.

This was his last time out and he wanted to remember everything about it: Hammer Jones got moody and tuned his guitar over and over. Lorna Williams got on social media and told the world who she was playing with and where. That's why she was going places, J thought. Well, one of the reasons. It helps being incredibly talented, he supposed.

Some of these places have a guy who shows up on show nights to do sound. Especially places like The Marshes where the stage is used for theater. Tonight the performers were left alone, which meant doing their own sound. None of them minded. It was simple.

Lorna went to the back of the room and sat at the board while J stood up and sang a song from his record.

"Sounds good," she said, "no need to adjust anything."

Hammer declined to sound check. Gruffly suggesting that if the great J Kamer thought it was okay, it was surely good enough for a ridiculous little performer like him.

With that, all the prep work was done ninety minutes early. The three sat down and talked about lineup. Since it was J's last show, Lorna thought he should be the closer, that meant her giving up her spot, so she should at least get to go second. That left Hammer to open. He was disgusted by this.

"Is that what you think of me? I'm last place here? I'm the opening act, and you two just assume I'm fine with that."

"Dan," said J, bypassing the stage name which was a small *faux pas*, "let's be real honest. What have either of us really done in the last forty years?"

"Don't do that to yourself. You put out that album, and it was a hell of an album."

"What did it go to on the charts?"

"I mean... you know it didn't chart..."

"Precisely."

"So? So what? That's not the measure of an artist."

"You're right. That's true. It's not the measure of an artist. But the artist still has to eat somehow."

"So what, the almighty dollar wins for you?"

"It does for you, mister corner office."

"That's...that's different..."

"No, that's life. Everybody's got to survive somehow. I'm surviving. But I'm not thriving. I'm too old to be riding buses to shows. But I can't afford a car. At sixty! There's a term for that and it's 'poor planning.'"

"Say what you will, J, but at least I can say I never turned my back on my friends," Hammer said. He turned around and walked out of the bar.

Lorna stepped forward. She'd been silent since it became clear something about all of this was personal between the two men, "I guess it goes without saying he's upset about you quitting."

"Right, I think he thinks I'm abandoning him and judging him and making fun all at once."

"Are you sure you're not?" she asked.

"I uh, well damn," J would have instinctively said no, but Hammer wouldn't have said so, "Let me think on that," he said. He knew his situation was such that he had to give up the road. It was too late in life to really start a career. Finding a dream income wasn't really a motivation for him. Just something with a bit less wear and tear on the shoulders. If it wasn't too much for the universe to spare, maybe something a bit more dignified.

Staying on the road was a non starter, but there had to be a way to get through to Hammer too. There was no sense in losing a friend over quitting.

The show got going with Hammer Jones' set. He had an easy, digestible folk style. He made statements in songs, but they were common statements and he added little to them. The audience had not much reaction to these. What was controversial twenty years ago now seemed obvious to folks. The impact wasn't the same. He had some sprawling ballads that really seemed to resonate with the audience. And he closed with a big energetic number about dismantling the electoral college.

Lorna Williams took the stage next and the energy in the room changed. The people really focused on what she was doing. What she did was express her range. There were low pensive minimalist songs, high energy catchy songs, ballads, and a song about the gender bias in hiring practices of northern Ohio manufacturing companies that informed, moved, and managed not to be a stale sentiment. One must admit it was a novel topic.

Then J took the stage. He felt like all the blood fell out of his body, the old nerves returned just like they did every time.

He started with a series of songs about growing up poor and having the world look down on you. Next, he spoke to the audience, "Tonight is a special night for me. I'm honored to share tonight with all of you, and Hammer Jones and Lorna Williams. I just met Lorna today. Hammer and I go way back. We've spent a lot of time together, bouncing ideas off one another, writing songs. Some really great songs were written by the two of us," he said leading into a song they had written together.

He followed it with another song they had collaborated on, and then another. He closed his set that night having played every single song that they worked on.

It was a deeply personal set, and the audience sensed that. They were invested, they hung on every note and were forgiving of any miscues. J closed the show and thanked them. He had not had an audience's buy-in so strongly in a long time.

He set his guitar on his case and came off the stage looking for Hammer. The audience was leaving their seats and filing out into the bar. They said kind words to J as he tried to push through.

"That was great, man," a voice said.

"I really enjoyed that," said another.

He felt he should be gracious and thank them for saying so, but also he wanted them to cease to be impediments to finding his friend. He settled on a very clipped "Thank you," and forged ahead.

He found Hammer Jones sitting in the back row staring emptily into space.

"What'd you think?"

"What the hell was that?"

"My last set. I dedicated it to a friend," he said trying to measure how well he'd smoothed things over.

"So, you play all the songs we wrote together and that's supposed to, what? Erase the fact that you're giving up? That you're abandoning me?"

"Come on, Dan. What do you want from me?"

"How about this: how about when you decide to quit and see it's painful, you don't go ahead and rub salt in the open wound by highlighting the exact reason why it's painful? How's that?"

"Listen, I'm sorry. But I can't keep doing this. It doesn't make sense financially like I said. Either way though I don't think it's a big enough thing to lose a friend over."

"Maybe you're overestimating the significance of our friendship."

"Obviously not if you're this pissed off."

"Go to hell, J," Hammer said. He stood up and walked away.

Lorna, who had been hanging back with a stranger stepped forward now, "Everything okay?"

J looked at her and shook his head, "He's still upset from before."

"I might be able to help," she said.

"I don't know."

"This is Rick Rigley," she gestured to her companion, "He owns the record label that signed me. He wants to talk to you."

"Oh, nice to meet you Mr. Rigley."

"Call me Rick. J, that was a fantastic set. Your lyrical content is amazing! We'd be very interested in a deal with you to put out your next record. And I could give you an advance of five thousand dollars."

"A record?" J said.

"Sure! Based on what I saw tonight, you've got the goods and I can't wait to see what it sounds like when you're done."

"They're good people to work with," Lorna said, "I got a really good deal on my contract and rights and everything. It's legit."

"You don't have to answer right now, you can think it over for a few days."

"Oh I don't need to think it over, Mr. Rigley. I'm old and poor and ridiculous and I'm done. I'm done playing, performing, recording, all of it."

"Oh," said Mr. Rigley, "but I thought..."

"I don't care, Rick. Go to hell."

J didn't even collect his guitar or suitcase. He just walked straight back to the bus station and waited alone for the long empty ride home.

The Pillars Getaway

Everett's bed and breakfast filled with the smell of oatmeal cookies. He was preparing for the second day of the historical society's annual getaway. He set the cookies out on a cooling rack, poured himself a cup of coffee and waited for his houseguests to emerge. Everett was generally enthused, as a person. He was a permanent beacon of positive energy, it seemed. He would sit and endlessly listen to local singer/songwriters at coffee shops, no matter how bad they were, and beam with pride at each stanza. He couldn't honestly claim to be interested in any one thing more than any other. He was simply fascinated by it all. So, he cheerfully hosted events like the Pillars Getaway as often as he could.

Darlene Stoneweather had made an impression the night before at the welcoming dinner. She did not give one solid damn about the Clapford Historical Society, and she wanted that to be known by all. The impression she'd made on Everett, though he didn't like to admit it, was that she was rude. She was, nevertheless, perfectly playing the role played by many women of her stature in Southern Indiana: convinced her time was more valuable than whatever your project was, come what may. Never mind she had chosen to be there, and if her time was being wasted, she was the one responsible.

There was this Mason Mathis fellow who was in some tenuous way connected to the Clapfords, *the* Clapfords, mind you. Mason was sure the connection itself was of historical interest, if only the Society would allow him a little time to explain it. To date he had encountered little success. Everett watched and admired his eagerness the night before as he tried to be involved in the general conversation time after time in spite of being routinely shunned.

Then there was Marietta Vanworthy, a local historical society dignitary. While not especially invested in the particulars of any event or topic of historical interest, she always seemed to know the general thrust of any story. She was like someone who knew how to get you to any neighborhood but couldn't find a gas station once they got there. She could tell you any story about Clapford County, unless you wanted details.

The Pillars Getaway was an exclusive annual event. The purpose of the event was to identify a new theme for the Historical Society to pursue for the following year. The theme helped funnel all the efforts of the CHS into a common direction. Without the theme there was chaos, everyone working on their own pet projects generating a lot of noise and static. A theme turned it all into a melody that could be appreciated by everyone.

The Getaway was also a fundraising opportunity inasmuch as the event was pay to play. This year Marietta was the only official society member who had sufficient personal funds to make the donation and pay for the bed and breakfast.

This year Marietta felt as though they were rather scraping the bottom of the barrel. Darlene Stoneweather held no interest to or for local history. She was on the invite list simply for the donation. Darlene accepted solely for the optics of the thing: to be seen giving a damn about—and a check to—local history. This was legwork she was doing in preparation for a run at the Hardy town council. For her, the weekend was transactional, political, and damned inconvenient. Marietta knew she was hardly going to supply a renewed sense of purpose to the CHS.

Then there was Mason Mathis. He had made some sort of claim about his ancestor's connection to county history, and the Society had to listen, now that he had paid his way in to the Getaway. He had the faint scent of credibility due to his founding of the Acorn Museum up in Bedford. None of the other wild tales in the suggestion pile were written by a museum founder. Even if the museum's brochure did boast about its display of "interesting nuts."

Marietta shuddered when she thought of it.

Everett was imagining the interesting conversations his guests might have as he waited for them in the dining room. He imagined some revelation from this weekend re-shaping Clapford County's self-image. There would be press of course, and he would modestly inform the newspaper he was a mere fly on the wall at the critical moment of revelation. Of course they'd pressure him for more details. "No, no," he said aloud, "they're the real heroes here. I just served the tea."

"You served tea?" Marietta asked him. She'd only just come into the room. Everett realized he'd been caught talking to himself and paled. Marietta was a serious person, she spoke in quick even-toned bursts. Some listeners felt she was harsh and curt when she spoke, but there was no emotional rebuke in her voice. Everything was logical and rational. After years of enduring the workplace, a sort of free-floating rationale of making subtle changes to avoid unpleasantness had gradually found this manner of speech to be an effective means of survival.

She would not have chosen it for herself, it was entirely shaped by the reactions of others, and she was not entirely conscious of it as it was happening to her. But now it was engrained, and there was little reason to change it.

"I can make tea if you prefer, but coffee is ready this morning. Over in the decanter in the counter," Everett said.

"And the tea?"

"Darjeeling, chamomile, Earl Grey, Irish breakfast."

"Coffee it is," she said as she turned to the counter.

"Those teas aren't...your cup of tea?" Everett laughed loudly as if the joke were the greatest invention ever.

"No," Marietta responded humorlessly.

"How did you sleep?"

"It was fine, Everett."

Everett was familiar with Marietta from previous events, but still felt that a little humor would go a long way towards easing his embarrassment from having her walk in while he was talking to himself. He found some comfort in telling himself she must have only captured the rote empirical fact that he was speaking aloud and the content of his speech. She was far too busy and important to take note of social mores against speaking to oneself in the empty dining room of one's own bed and breakfast.

Darlene and Mason came down at the same time. The four of them sat around the breakfast table in a polite but austere silence. Ordinarily, the order of the day on the Getaway was that each participant would make a proposal to the committee for what the theme should be for the coming year. This year Marietta had no suggestions, and Darlene was not interested, so the day was to be spent traveling to a site where Mason was going to be making his proposal.

"What is this great find of yours?" Darlene asked Mason.

"Oh all will be revealed in due time," he responded coyly.

Marietta answered, "With all due respect, you're taking us all on a little bit of a drive through the country, we'd like to know something about it."

"Fair enough," Mason said, "I can tell you I am going to prove a claim that was made before and disproved."

"Hmm," Darlene said. It sounded tedious to her.

"And you're taking us to Buffalo Bluff. I'm stumped," Marietta said.

Mason just smiled.

"You've got your work cut out for you," Marietta said.

"What happened when it was disproved before?" Everett asked.

Mason jumped in, eager to take control of the narrative, "Some good evidence was presented badly, and some other good evidence was buried, and the whole claim was dismissed."

"What claim, though?"

"All in good time," Mason said.

They piled in Everett's car and he drove them to Buffalo Bluff. Along the way they passed beautiful Southern Indiana scenery: ever-present rolling hills that refused to admit even the suggestion of flat land; winding roads that arched sweepingly from right to left and then back again for reasons completely lost to time; fields with the five o'clock shadow of harvested corn and beans, now hibernating after giving all they could for the year; the woods that began at the bottom of hills in the creek beds where sycamores flourished with their haunting white trunks and branches. From there the woods ran uphill through oaks, poplars, walnut trees, and the occasional cedar spotting the landscape with a splash of green. The lifelessness of the land and trees made the light seem grey. Yet there was something gorgeous about it. It was a dead spooky world that promised to return to glory in the spring.

They saw eight or ten wild turkeys in a field, a pair of deer just daring to peer out of the wood line, and several small herds of cattle at various farms. It was a half-hour drive and Everett rejoiced in small ways at every sight along the way. The picturesque end of fall seemed to connect him to the land in a new way. He felt the rhythm of the land, the grand cycle that repeats each year. He was honored to be among people who lived in such a connected way to this grand inexorable pattern, and to be preserving and celebrating the history of this cyclical way of life. All of the universe came together and presented itself to him, he thought. Everything made sense to him and he was contented by it.

He was deep in this joyous silent reverie when Darlene shattered it by asking "Is it much further?"

"Just at the top of this next hill. Buffalo Bluff."

"Mmm," she said annoyed.

Mason had a singular look of eager anticipation, as if he had only to get to the right place, take the right action, and his life would thenceforth be complete and perfect.

Buffalo Bluff was named as a site along the famous Buffalo Trace trails that ranged from salt licks in Kentucky and ran through Indiana into Illinois. These were trails that bison once ranged over. At the top of a hill in what would become Clapford County, a hunter who had been tracking the buffalo had set up his camp a little early in the evening due to having been winded from climbing the hill. Before nightfall, two or three other hunters joined him and set up nearby. In the morning before taking off down the trail again, even more folks stopped at the site. For a week or so, there was a continuous chain of hunters camped on the site. The place developed a reputation as a stopping ground for hunters. One young man set up a store on top of the hill, and gradually a small community developed around the campground and became known as Buffalo Bluff.

As the Pillars Getaway arrived in the little town they noticed a sign on the city limits that said, "Welcome to Buffalo Bluff, a city that defiantly sleeps." This slogan was intended by the locals as a thumbing of the nose at New York City, which they saw as the epitome of coastal elitism. New York is known as the city that never sleeps, and as a rejection of all things New Yorker, the town decided to emphatically state that they do sleep here. It was a rejection of a way of life that they saw as oppressive, although it only existed hundreds of miles away, and had little to no impact on their lives. Still they courageously posted their sign: hidden away in the woods in a tiny southern Indiana village where it could not have had less effect.

The intention behind the sign was lost on nearly all visitors. Most just wondered at the optimistic use of the word "city." The town itself was a few houses on a main road, a general store, and a post office. Much of the town's population lived In outlying areas nestled in the woods.

The town was completely surrounded by woods save one two-hundred meter stretch of the main road, the trees fell away and revealed a majestic view of rolling hills of forest. It was a popular site to visit during the fall, when the leaves change color and the entire landscape blazed in glorious oranges, reds and yellows.

Mason directed Everett to a part of the woods just outside of the town. The decaying remains of a small house were there, and there was an old shed as well, the roof of which was completely crumpled under the weight of history and dead leaves. Mason led the group over to the shed.

"An ancestor of mine once lived here in Clapford County. Although he lived down in Hardy where we came from. His name was Josiah Mathis. His wife my great-great- —not sure how many greats—grandmother Myffanwy was the object of admiration of Walter Clapford."

"I've never heard of her," Marietta said.

"Me either," Darlene chimed in.

"No, you wouldn't have," Mason said, "Walter staged a bank robbery on his own bank, and pinned it on Josiah so that he could get rid of him. The town had Josiah executed so he wouldn't be a problem for Walter Clapford."

"Sir, that is an incredible accusation! You are speaking about a revered, founding father of this town. The county is named after him. Their family is still very much around and in a position of influence."

"Yes, it's true, I know. But Myffanwy had to flee the town and leave her family behind to get away from this place. My family was robbed of a place here. Our family name has been tarnished for almost two hundred years."

"I assure you not only is it not tarnished, we've never heard of it," Darlene said.

"Precisely my point," Mason said, "You don't know this story about your own town. What more appropriate project for the historical society to take on?"

"Can you prove any of this?" Marietta asked.

Everett spoke up, "Why are we in Buffalo Bluff?"

"Yes, why are we here?" Darlene asked.

"The evidence against Josiah presented in court was that a certain red wagon was seen at the bank at the time of the robbery: the bank really was robbed by the way. That same wagon was supposed to have been seen at Josiah's farm. The problem is, there wasn't exactly a wide variety of places to get a wagon back then. All of the ones around here came from the same man, and he painted them all the same way, so they could be recognized as his handiwork out in the world."

"Is that the evidence?"

"Well no of course not. That would only prove they *could* have been wrong. I aim to prove they were wrong in fact."

"And how will you do that?" Marietta asked.

"Because the wagon from the bank robbery is underneath this shed, where it was taken right after the robbery, and never moved again, for fear of being spotted and connected with the crime Josiah Mathis was already killed for committing."

"How can you prove that?" Marietta asked, "As you say all the wagons around here looked the same. How could you know this was the one, two hundred years later?"

"Because the money is still in it, still in the bank bags."

"WHAT?" Darlene shouted.

"They didn't want to be seen suddenly having a lot of money right after the robbery, so they left it hidden under this shed. There was a little secret stowaway room down there. Then the support beam collapsed and they couldn't get in the room. They no longer felt safe going in there, and maybe they felt some guilt as well. Maybe they thought the beam snapping was divine retribution. I'm guessing a little bit here, but the fact remains they never touched it, through five generations, until this one. One of them finally felt like they could help clear a man's name and ease the collective conscience of their own family at the same time."

"So they called you?" Marietta asked.

"They called me. It took a while to find me, but they did."

Everett was ecstatic, "That's incredible! So now the Historical Society can pick this up and clear your ancestor's name!"

"Hold on. We need to think about this," Darlene said, suddenly very interested in the weekend, "I'm running for office in this county next year. I don't want my name attached to something that is going to take down the county founder's reputation."

"But the truth is the truth," said Everett.

"I agree we should be careful," said Marietta, "this story alleges that Walter Clapford was a womanizer, and conspired to frame a man and have him executed just to keep a woman available to him. A *married* woman at that!"

"Not just that," said Mason, "He used his newspaper to turn public opinion against the man too. He took away his life and his name."

"But now you want to take away Mr. Clapford's name. The name of our county...imagine the 'Clapford Historical Society' promoting a narrative that takes down Mr. Clapford, and his descendants are still very much around and in good standing. We must think of them also."

Darlene was growing nervous. She clearly didn't care for this kind of talk. Anything that might upset the Clapford family was bad for her campaign, "I just don't think it's fair to those folks who live in this community for an outsider to drudge up the past and paint them in a bad light."

Mason looked disgusted, "The people in this community, you said. The people who live here matter more than the people who don't to you, eh?"

"Well now, I didn't say that exactly," she said.

"What about the folks who would be in this community if they hadn't been ran out of town? Don't they matter?"

"Of course, of course. I am simply saying we have to be sensitive to the feelings of people who live here and not let outsiders needlessly upset them."

Everett was deflated, "I think we should head back to the bed and breakfast for lunch," he offered.

They rode back in silence, each one strategizing for the discussion that was surely coming. Everett looked at the stubble fields but this time he did not find himself connected to the land or proud to be among the folks who lived by its cycle. He saw obstinance and pettiness. He saw an unwillingness to change or to confront reality. Even the scenery lost its picturesque aspect. He didn't like feeling this way, and he was saddened by the loss of his drive time ritual.

When they arrived back at Everett's bed and breakfast the guests each went to their rooms to think while Everett made lunch. This was technically outside his normal scope of activity, but he always provided meals for the Getaway, it was part of their fee for the weekend.

Cooking pepped him back up. He was back to singing and whistling and imagining talking with reporters again in no time. In his kitchen he was lord of the realm, and he felt energized by the way it all went as he planned in there.

He was in quite a bouncy mood when lunch was served at one o'clock. The four sat down together and began talking about the proposal while they ate.

"Darlene had a marvelous suggestion, Mason, that I think will work for everyone," Marietta said.

"Oh what was that?" asked Everett.

"We could pick up this question of who robbed the bank back in eighteen-whatever-it-was, and focus on the fact that the wrong fella was accused and convicted. But we don't pick up any of the things you said about Walter Clapford. We clear your ancestor's name without tearing down anyone else's name in the process," Darlene said. She marveled at herself, and what a fine politician she was becoming: taking in the concerns of others and finding a solution that would keep everybody happy. She was beaming.

"That's not justice," Mason said, shattering Darlene's reverie, "It's not the truth."

"It's not false, we'd be saying everything true about Josiah Mathis not being a bank robber," Darlene offered.

"But you'd be hiding the rest of the story. I don't like it, it's a cover-up," Mason said.

Everett was back to dismay. He had hoped a little quiet time in their rooms and a nice lunch would settle this matter. He felt that this hope had been naïve now.

Marietta chimed in, "Unfortunately we have to negotiate the optics of the thing, the politics of the situation. We can't just say whatever's true. There are more considerations on the table. As the Clapford Historical Society, we cannot invest time or money in a project that will mar the image of the county's founder. It will be as bad as when we commissioned that man to write out the stories of Clapford County, and nothing ever came of it. You want to get the whole thing out in order to not only clear your ancestor's name, but fully explain why it happened the way it did. I can understand that. But if we can't compromise on this, we may be at an impasse."

"You're saying you can't support this research then?"

"If you can't bend then, yes, that is what I am saying."

"I can't bend."

"Then I think you have your answer from us, I'm afraid."

Darlene was a little relieved. If her solution wasn't being taken up, the second-best outcome was to not damage her chances of being elected.

Mason was defiant, "Well then, someone else will support it, and it will come out anyway."

"I can see you're determined, and for what it's worth I do think it should come out. It just can't be supported by this group. I hope you see that," Marietta said.

"I do, thank you. I'll find funding elsewhere."

"What about from me?" Everett asked.

"You?" Marietta asked.

"The important thing is to get the truth out there."

"Well I agree, but I'm afraid it will mean the CHS can no longer be affiliated with your business. Besides, who knows how the Clapfords will react."

Everett thought about this, he thought about how he felt on the drive home, and he thought about poor Mason's great great granny. He looked steadily at Marietta and said, "So be it."

Everett turned to Mason feeling a new purpose, "What do you say Mr. Mathis? Shall we boldly tell the truth and never think twice about the consequences?"

"I accept," said Mason.

The following year, in a peer-reviewed periodical there was a scarcely noticed paper published explaining the Josiah Mathis story. The feared reaction from the Clapfords never came. One doubts they ever heard about the paper to react to it. Everett's business did not dry up. He never regained his feeling of connection to the people around him, but he felt a new calm and pride as he drove through the country.

The historical society missed his bed and breakfast only one year before coming back to its home. There he casually directed the attendees' attention to a framed journal article in his lobby and invited them to make history during their stay.

Printed in Great Britain
by Amazon

60213348R00144